THE
HONORABLE
PRISON

THE
HONORABLE
PRISON
Lyll Becerra de Jenkins

LODESTAR BOOKS   E. P. DUTTON   NEW YORK

The first two chapters of this book originally appeared
in slightly altered form in *The New Yorker.*

Library of Congress Cataloging-in-Publication Data

Jenkins, Lyll Becerra de.
  The honorable prison / Lyll Becerra de Jenkins.
  p. cm.
  "Lodestar books."
  Summary: Because of the moral stand taken by her father,
a newspaper editor who has persistently attacked the military
dictator ruling their Latin American country, Marta and her
family find themselves prisoners of the government.
  ISBN 0-525-67238-9
  [1. Political prisoners—Latin America—Fiction. 2. Latin
America—Fiction. 3. Freedom of speech—Fiction.] I. Title.
PZ7. J414HO   1987
[Fic]—dc19   87-25197
                                              CIP
Published in the United States by E. P. Dutton,   AC
2 Park Avenue, New York, N.Y. 10016,
a division of NAL Penguin Inc.

Published simultaneously in Canada by
Fitzhenry & Whiteside Limited, Toronto

Editor: Rosemary Brosnan

Printed in the U.S.A.   W   First Edition
10 9 8 7 6 5 4 3 2 1

to the memory
of my parents

1

September 1955. THURSDAY, FULL MOON, reads the calendar at the front of the classroom.

Today is a day like any other day. From inside the convent we hear police whistles, shooting, the wailing of an ambulance siren, and silence. The sounds follow one another in the same order—a choreography that takes place in our city three, four, and more times a day.

Sister Tekla, who has been explaining about the heroes who offered their lives to free our country from the Spaniards' domination, interrupts herself. My classmates look at me, and I wonder, whom did they shoot today? Did the military police discover the secret place where my father and his friends gather daily to print their newspaper? Will I see my father this evening?

Last week they shot the father of the Julián twins as he crossed a street not far from the convent. "An unknown assailant shot the journalist Nicolás Julián," the official press said. "Major Vicente Pineda, Chief of the Police Department, will pursue a careful investigation." This is how the government reports its own crimes.

Señor Julián owned our country's most important radio station. He was a close friend of my father.

1

Relatives of the Julián girls came to the convent to pick them up after the crime. I saw them leaning against each other, their mouths opened, as though they were choking on silent screams. With their long, slender necks, the identical twins resembled two wounded swans.

"They will not come back for the rest of the term," Mother Andrea, the principal, said. "We must pray for them."

"Pray for your father, Marta!" Mother Andrea told me the other day. "Fanaticism is a form of madness that destroys all that is noble in man."

When I told my father, he smiled and said, "So Bishop Vargas is coaching the good nuns, eh?" Bishop Vargas is a close friend of the dictator.

It's impossible to resume history class while the siren and the police whistles continue. Now Sister Tekla raises her arms in frustration. "This is the third interruption today!" Then, as if perhaps she had said something improper, she quickly adds, "Let us take advantage of the situation. Open your books and study."

The convent, an old castle built by a Spanish viceroy for his mistress, had been my second home. As a small girl, I would run through its long, narrow corridors, searching for secret passages, imagining that I saw the ghosts of the conquistadors. Now, as I walk the corridors of the convent, the nuns scatter from my path like crows taking flight.

The daughters of high-ranking military men have become dictators within the convent. Even the nuns fear them. There are three in my senior class: Graciela, Esperanza, and Maria Isabel. Early in the term, Graciela said, "Marta, you get A's on your compositions. Here, write mine!" Shortly thereafter, I was writing compositions for Graciela's friends as well. Sister Tekla assigned us the same subject week after week—

Our General. "Write a brief biography describing his outstanding qualities," she would tell us. Or, "In two pages, point out the similarities between our General and Simón Bolívar."

"Our General," I would write, and then my pen would stop. "Our General . . ." I would sit staring at the blank page for hours, until I hit upon a trick. Copying from editorials in the official press, I was able to fill pages by changing the language slightly. "Our General is ahead of his time," one editorial said. I wrote, "Our General is a man with vision." My brother Ricardo joined in the game. He imitated the handwriting of the girl whose homework I was doing and wrote, "Our General is infallible, like the Pope." We giggled, imagining the reaction of the nuns.

"In an exemplary gesture of democracy, our General invited some university students to participate in an open dialogue," another official editorial said. Papa had told us the truth about this event. "It was the usual, a dialogue between students and bayonets!" "In a gesture of generosity," I wrote for Graciela's composition, "Our General invited the university students to join him in a frank conversation. It's too bad the students didn't appreciate this privilege. They were disrespectful to our General. Ten students are dead; several lie wounded in the hospital. It's expected that other students will learn from this lesson." After that, the requests for compositions stopped.

My father had been a friend of the General. In those days, he was often invited to come to the convent to speak to us. Mother Andrea would ask me to wait for him at the entrance hall and to escort him to the auditorium.

Papa would always come wearing a red carnation in his lapel, while the pockets of his jacket bulged with papers and a thick notebook.

As we walked through the corridors to the auditorium, he waltzed. "Come, Marta," he'd say, placing my hand on top of his as if we were dancing a minuet. I followed his step, laughing nervously, turning to make sure that there were no nuns watching.

At the door of the auditorium, he patted his bulging pockets, flicked the carnation, and winked at me. We walked in to the chorus of *"¡Buenas tardes, Don Miguel!"*

Mother Andrea was all smiles as she advanced quickly toward my father. Her habit swirled; the rosary around her waist clicked. The nun was as effusive as a cocker spaniel greeting its owner.

"Thank you for coming, Don Miguel, thank you!" she repeated, leading him to the platform at the front of the room, where there was a table with a crystal pitcher of papaya juice.

But even in those days, Papa disappointed the nuns. Perhaps he did not praise their efforts enough; perhaps he was too outspoken. Somehow Papa failed to fulfill the nuns' expectations.

I recall the last time. He spoke against a costly new monument in Parque de la Independencia. The monument was not only unnecessary, he said; it was an affront in a city where children sleep in the streets and beggars crowd the aisles of churches. "We are obsessed with statues. Our city is like a woman who throws a garish dress over underwear that is soiled and ragged."

Mother Andrea was startled. "Señor Maldonado," she said as he was leaving, "your comparison, I mean our girls are very impressionable."

"Good, Mother Andrea. We are in great need of impressionable people!"

He was not invited back to the convent.

One evening during dinner, my father announced to

Mama, Ricardo, and me that he was launching a campaign against the General.

"Did you really believe, Miguel, that the General was going to be different from other politicians?" Mama asked.

"I believed in him, yes, Margarita, and made others believe in him. I will rectify my error."

Shortly afterward, his newspaper was closed by the government. The paper, however, continues to circulate underground. My father and his friends gather daily in a secret place to print *La Tribuna* on a small private press.

Now the bell is ringing. The halls fill with the shuffling feet of girls getting in line to leave.

On our way to the entrance hall, we sing,

> March on, march on for liberty
> Justice will triumph.

"I want to hear everyone," Sister Petronila says. "Come on, girls, everybody!" She claps her pudgy hands. And we sing,

> Libertyyyy . . . Justiiice . . .

My father is at the door of the convent. I rejoice at the sight of him alive but wonder why he has come to walk me home.

He takes my arm. We do not cross the park in front of the convent building, which shortens our way home. Instead, he leads me along the block. As we move on, I find myself thinking I should not walk too close to Papa, so that if they shoot at him, it will not hit me. Abruptly I disengage my arm from his grip to lag behind. But almost immediately I draw closer to him again and put my arm under his. He turns to look at my arm, which does not stop trembling.

We walk for a while in silence. We are now on Avenida

Libertador. I am not afraid anymore. It is in parks and deserted streets where they shoot and kidnap people.

At the corner I notice Don Ramón Villa, a neighbor. He looks away from my father and me, pretending to be absorbed in a store window.

"We'll leave Thursday at midnight," Papa now says softly. He had to hurry his plans, he explains, and tells me about Don José Lopez, his assistant at the newspaper. "He was dragged out of his home two nights ago."

He hushes my cry, which makes two women turn. We do not speak for a moment.

Don José and his wife played croquet with my parents on Sunday afternoons. I can still see the four of them in our backyard. Mama and Doña Elvira, taller than their husbands, both women wearing skirts and silk blouses, Mama with a bright scarf on her head. My father and Don José, with dark suits and vests, looking gray and paternal. They move awkwardly in contrast to the agile, laughing women, who win most of the games.

"Where are we going, Papa?"

"To the border. Then across it. Getting visas is out of the question!"

People are pouring out of buildings. Cinemas and cafés are closing. Although it is still early, the panic that precedes the sound of the siren announcing curfew is descending over the city.

"Taxi! Taxi!" cries a couple with a child, but the cars speed by, ignoring shouts and signals. Military jeeps are already patrolling the streets. Two officers jump out of a police car, and there are soldiers installing themselves everywhere along the *avenida*—their rifles pointing at the rushing crowd. It's a day like any other day.

Only the beggars remain at the doors of buildings and lie

in corners. "Alms, for the love of God!" wails a woman with a child wrapped in tatters.

We leave the avenue to walk toward our street. My eyes are on the house at the end of the block. I am looking at the roses in front of my mother's sewing room and at Ricardo's bedroom window, where the curtains do not stir. I am thinking of the relatives of the dictator's enemies who disappear or are taken to jail every day. My father's eyes are also fixed on our house. We move faster.

⧉ 2

My father is in his study, next to the foyer, where I sit. I listen to his cough and his typewriter, two sounds that have been the background of my growing years.

Ricardo snaps cards on the living room rug, playing solitaire, and upstairs Mama moves about, her heels a quick drumming on the ceiling above me.

The suitcases are ready in the foyer. We have packed "the essentials," Mama kept repeating—some of our clothes and linens.

Will we be able to leave tonight? I imagine I hear the answer to my question in the *clack-clack* of my father's old Remington, Yes-No-Yes, the *click* of my brother's cards, and the *tap-tap* of Mama's heels, No-Yes-No-No.

A military policeman is stationed around the clock at the corner of our street. He is there to watch every move of "the journalist enemy of the General." We have been a threat to the neighbors since Papa began writing editorials against the dictator. But before, these same neighbors used to say that Miguel Maldonado's family gave prestige to our street.

There's a knock at the front door. I give a start, and for a moment all sounds in the house stop. Then Papa calls me,

"Marta, are you there? Open the door; it's Juan Hernández."

My father's friend, a short man with a black toothbrush moustache, comes in. He greets me absentmindedly, patting my shoulder, looking from his watch to the grandfather clock. He hangs his hat on the rack but keeps his overcoat on.

"Perfect timing, Juan," Papa says, coming out of the study, rearranging the pages he has been typing. "Come in." He turns back to the study.

"It's all here, Miguel!" Hernández says, smiling, opening his overcoat and tapping the breast pocket of his suit. "Right here!"

"Who is it?" Mother calls from upstairs.

"I'll be leaving in five minutes, Margarita!" Hernández pauses to answer, then follows Papa into the study.

Ricardo bursts out of the living room. "See, Marta, we are ready to leave!" He runs upstairs, two steps at a time.

I envy his excitement. I know Papa is referring to the typed pages in his hand, no doubt his last attack on the General before leaving. The article will appear in his newspaper, which will continue circulating underground with Hernández's supervision.

They are speaking in low voices. I want to hear a word about us tonight, something to reassure myself that my father's first concern is our safety.

"Miguel, you think only of your struggle." Mama's reproach of these past months comes to my mind. "Always your beliefs, and this time at your family's expense!"

The study door opens. Hernández comes out first. Both seem unaware of my presence in the foyer as they pass by and stand near the stairs. For a moment they nod and keep nodding, as though in a silent summing-up of what they just whispered in the study. Then they gaze somberly at the floor. Looking at them—Hernández in his bulky overcoat, my father in his gray poncho—I have the feeling that they are growing smaller, that they are shrinking.

Papa says at last, "Margarita, come down, dear. Juan wants to say good-bye."

My mother appears on the stairs at once. There's a glow to her paleness that matches the luster of the pearls she's wearing. I notice how thin she has grown. Her dark hair, combed into a high chignon, overwhelms the pretty face that looks pointed, angular, like a piece of sculpture that has been carved to excess.

For an instant I delude myself into thinking that all is normal, and Señor Hernández will be our dinner guest. At the table he will talk of his daughter and grandson and will discuss the state of our country with Papa while Ricardo and I bite our lips to keep from laughing at his constant "definitely," "infinitely," "absolutely." But Mama's eyes, as she gazes from my father to Hernández, bring me back to reality. It is easy to guess her unspoken question. "Will it be all right tonight?"

"*Tranquila,* Margarita," Hernández says, raising his arm to shake her hand. "It's all taken care of. Have no fear."

"Juan and I just went briefly over the whole thing, Margarita, step by step," Papa adds.

Her face lightens. With sudden animation, she comes down the last steps.

"You must go now, Juan!" Papa takes Hernández's hat from the rack. We all look at the grandfather clock. Soon the siren will announce curfew. There's an insistent honking of the traffic rushing by outside.

Papa and his friend embrace. "*¡Hasta pronto, Miguel!*" Hernández takes Mama's hand in both of his, then moves to pat my shoulder, but instead shakes my hand. "Adios, Martica." He waves to Ricardo, whom I notice only now, standing at the top of the stairs. My brother's is the only smiling face.

"I'll see you soon, Miguel, I'm sure, absolutely sure. It's a matter of a few months, maybe weeks," Hernández says, lifting his arm as if he were pronouncing a public speech, his voice quivering on the last words.

"Careful, Juan. Go up to Avenida Libertador and move with the crowd, fast!"

Hernández hurries out.

"Be careful, Juan," my parents say at the same time.

The front door closes with a bang. We stand still, our eyes on the spot where Hernández was a minute before. Clearing his throat and without looking at us, my father returns to the study.

I help Mama to serve dinner, a casserole of rice, beef, and tomatoes. Our maid, Ana, left this week. "It's not safe for you to be with us, Ana," Mama explained. We wanted her out of our way for tonight's plan.

My mother keeps moving around the table, passing dishes one moment, dashing to the kitchen the next, in unnecessary activity.

Our dining room looks larger than usual this evening. The potted fern plants have been sent to Uncle Alberto and Aunt Lila's house, the china cabinet is empty, and there are no pictures on the walls—all the adornments around the house have been placed in a trunk.

Ricardo's eyes do not leave Papa as we eat. He is probably expecting to hear the usual amusing remarks that our father reserves for dinner hour, but tonight Papa is in a somber mood, the lines across his forehead etched more deeply.

"Where will we be tomorrow at this hour, Papa?"

11

For a moment Papa says nothing. "Tomorrow? Ah, yes . . . away from all this!" he answers finally.

Ricardo smiles, looking at me, then at Mama, but we go on eating.

"We must try to rest a few hours before we go so that—" but he doesn't finish the phrase.

"You've told us so little, Miguel!"

"It'll all be fine, Margarita." He pats her hand.

It was at dinnertime that we had expected to hear about tonight's plan. In this room we have always felt free to speak. In the rest of the house, we can hear noises from the street and the neighbors' radios, even their voices. Around this table Papa has had secret meetings with other journalists who, like him, opposed the dictator. Those nights the front door was left open for the men to come directly into the dining room. From the foyer Ricardo and I would watch them arriving, separately, wearing hats and bulky overcoats in which they hid folders and papers.

Some nights my father and his friends seemed animated, slapping each other's backs, laughing, as if they were at the brink of some exciting event.

"Marta, I think it's going to happen soon, maybe tomorrow, this week," Ricardo would whisper. "He'll be overthrown, the General."

From the foyer we could not hear what they said, but we were able to see them through the large window of the dining room, which faced the patio directly across the foyer. We would see them behind the glass as if we were watching actors in a silent movie. Mama would leave coffee and pastries on a card table in a corner, then rush to her bedroom and, with the light out, watch the street.

Because of the curfew, my father's friends stayed at our house talking all night. In the morning they made a somber group, with their dark overcoats and hats, shrouded in cigarette smoke, waiting by the door for the last patrol car to go by.

Then the nightly meetings stopped. The General changed the curfew hour from ten o'clock at night to six in the evening, and my father and his friends gathered in secret places during the day.

Now I see Mama clearing the table. I follow her to the kitchen, carrying a tray with dirty dishes.

She slips on an apron, and for a moment we fuss with pans and dishes without speaking.

"There are many helping us, friends of your father. Everything will be all right, Marta." She's handing me a clean plate to dry.

"I know!" I answer in the brusque manner I use when she guesses my thoughts. "I was just wondering who's going to look after our house."

She smiles, knowing that the house is not what's worrying me.

"Where are we going, Mama?"

"Your father and I were speaking the other night. He explained it won't be Venezuela with Pérez Jiménez or Paraguay with General Stroessner or Cuba with Batista. That it won't be Haiti or Guatemala, and you know, of course, it can't be the Dominican Republic with Trujillo. I don't know, Marta, but your father will tell us . . . tonight, I'm sure."

I go on drying dishes, wondering if the place where we are going makes any difference. All that matters is to be safe with my family. I become suddenly aware that the night around us has lost its sounds. There are no children running in their gardens, that bell-like quality of excitement in their voices as they play the last game before bed. There are no miaows of cats, no chirping of crickets, no faraway music of a radio. The police whistles, the shouts of *alto* (halt), even the silence of fear have turned us deaf to every other sound.

"Ah, yes, I almost forgot to tell you, Marta. There's good news about the newspaper building. Your father told me that the tobacco company renting it as a storage place has made an offer to buy the property."

"To buy the newspaper building?" And I want to add, And you call this good news? I cannot imagine my father without his newspaper.

Mama's voice goes on and on, but I am not listening.

It's Saturday morning. Papa, Ricardo, and I are walking on a narrow street in a sector to the south of the city. From parked trucks, drivers shout at one another, as if they are spitting silver arrows across the street. We smell leather and overripe fruits from a nearby open market. The owners of the leather stores along the block wear ponchos and cowboy hats. Rather than walk, they stamp in front of their shops, resembling flamenco dancers.

"Why do they walk like that, Papa?" Ricardo asks.

"They want to let everyone know that, although they come from tiny villages, they are not humble campesinos, that wearing shoes is not new to them."

The men fascinate me. A young one with a thin moustache and a fierce glance calls me señorita—"Buenos días, señorita."

Papa's building is at the end of the block—an old two-story house with a white tower like a dove on the red tile roof. The tower is my father's office.

The walls are lined with books: biographies of Bolívar, San Martín, José Echegaray; poems of José Asunción Silva, Nicanor Parra, Pablo Neruda; Russian and French novels, all poor editions from Argentina and Mexico, coming apart at the seams. My father handles them gently, as if they are wounded birds, his fingers trembling a bit as he leafs through them. Ricardo steals out of the office. "Don't bother anyone, Ricardo. Ask me what you want to know later."

I go to the window. The young man with the thin moustache is visiting the store across the street. I tell myself that he is there to see me, "la señorita Maldonado." I envision myself at the window: a dark beauty with long braids, Juliet in my father's white tower, but the glass windowpane reflects a skinny girl with short, curly hair.

"What's wrong, Marta, why did you knock at the window?"

"Money," Mama is now saying. "We need it. Your father has not earned a centavo since the government closed his newspaper. Our bank account has been steadily decreasing."

I turn my back to her and begin putting the silverware away. I don't want to pursue the subject. It's always like this with my mother. One moment she asks me not to worry; the next, she tells me her anxieties.

We are finished in the kitchen. Mama wipes the counter, hangs up her apron, and, sighing, looks about before she turns off the light.

My father and Ricardo are playing cards in the living room. As soon as we come in, Papa pushes aside the cards he is holding and pulls out a chair for Mama to sit down. I take the fourth chair around the card table, across from her.

"I want to explain a few things, Margarita, children." His voice is barely audible. "We are leaving at one fifty sharp. We'll walk up the street, each one carrying a suitcase. You're wondering about the soldier on the corner. He won't see us. It's all been arranged. On the next block, a sedan with an official license will be waiting for us. There is a very slim chance that a patrol car could go by. At that hour the men, particularly in this part of town, all go to sleep at their posts." He interrupts himself to cough. "We have good friends, and with their help I haven't overlooked any details. Please, Margarita, Marta, don't worry. It's going to be all right."

He is taking a thick bundle of bills out of his back pocket. "I gave Hernández power of attorney, and he withdrew our money from the bank at the last moment this afternoon. You take care of this, Margarita. Put it in your purse."

"All that money!"

"Don't shout, Ricardo!" Then, turning to Papa, Mama says, "But weren't they suspicious at the bank? Can we trust those people, Miguel?"

"Relax, Margarita. Everything has been considered. There's nothing unusual in withdrawing money from the bank. It's no secret to anyone that my paper has been closed by the government, that I need money, you see?"

We are away from the card table, standing around Papa.

"Remind me, Margarita, to take my capsules before one o'clock. Waking up the neighbors with my cough is something we must avoid." He says it half chuckling, as if it's a joke.

"You must take a rest now. Go up, the three of you. I'll read for a while."

We step out to the foyer, where we stand still for a moment. My mother is glancing toward the patio. "Did you and your friends, Miguel—were you aware that tonight is a full moon?"

"Of course, of course," he answers with ill-concealed irritation, walking toward his study.

Mama and Ricardo begin climbing the stairs. I say I'll be up shortly. I want to avoid my mother, who will whisper her fears and increase mine.

The soft music of a piano concerto is coming from the study. My father is moving along the book-lined wall, glancing at his books, touching one here, one there.

After a while he comes out and, kneeling on the floor, he pushes a dictionary into the suitcase with the Remington, which was packed after Hernández left. He winks at me. Mama has asked him to please stop sneaking books into the suitcases. Space should be reserved for last-minute things— she means his capsules and the tonics and syrups he must have daily.

I leaf through a magazine filled with photos of beauty queens—the Queen of Coffee, the Queen of the National Armada, the Queen of the Sea. I think of something my father said the other day: "Judging by what fills the censored press, our country is an example of unmitigated bliss: beauty queens, soccer games, and holy processions—useful news indeed to cover up the murders and disappearances that take place every day."

From time to time, a patrol car goes by. The siren of an ambulance wails in the distance, but the piano concerto has a soothing effect, and I am dozing off. I am suddenly in a tiny, square room with no windows and an iron door with bars. But in my dream I comfort myself: There's nothing alarming in dreaming about prison cells. Everyone who is against the government lives with two terrors: being shot or being imprisoned and tortured. Someone is knocking. I am remembering a novel I read where the prisoners conversed with one another by rapping on their cell walls. The pounding increases. And then I am awakened. Someone is banging at our front door. My father's hand is on my shoulder, pressing hard. He is standing near my chair.

"Who is it, what's happening, Papa?"

"Miguel, Miguel." Mama's voice is coming from upstairs.

"*Silencio,* shhh," he says, his eyes toward the patio, which is clearly outlined in the moonlight.

"Open the door, Señor Maldonado!" a man is yelling.

My father begins moving toward the corner with the suitcases but pauses midway. His body sags, as if he is slumping into an invisible chair.

"*Abra la puerta. ¡Abra!* Open the door!" There's more than one voice shouting now, and the hammering increases.

Papa removes his reading glasses and walks into the study to turn off the music. Then he walks to the entrance hall, calling, "*Un momento.*"

I hear the sound of the door opening, voices, boot steps, and the soft *clop* of my father's advancing slippers.

He is between two army officers, a major and a captain. The major touches his cap, bowing toward the stairs. Mama is standing at the bottom, clutching the banister rail.

My father has been reading a paper the officers gave him. He explains to Mama and me that the two officers have instructions to escort us out of the city. For an instant I believe that the two men are friends disguised as military men, and I think how cleverly it has all been planned by Papa and his friends. But I realize almost immediately that they are here to prevent us from getting away. My father's voice is calm, but I notice that the paper is shaking in his hand.

"It's the policy of our General to treat his enemies with benevolence," says the captain.

"Is it also the policy of your General to intrude on a family's privacy and to frighten women and children at midnight?"

"Miguel!" Mama calls. "I'll wake Ricardo." But she remains still, looking at the captain, who is now bending over, trying to open the bag with the Remington.

"There's no need to inspect!" the major says sharply, and, to my mother, "We'll take the suitcases out while you get ready, señora." He leaves the room briefly and returns with two soldiers.

Papa motions for me to go upstairs; then, with Papa holding Mama's arm, my parents follow me.

We move about the house quietly, avoiding looking at each other, picking up toiletries and my father's medications. I'm still dreaming, I say to myself. A sound like a whimper comes out of me, but I am not crying.

"¡Vamos, pronto, Señor Maldonado!" someone calls from downstairs. "It's a long way."

We walk down the stairs in single file, my father ahead. Ricardo's face is blank; he has not yet grasped what's going on.

Mama's dark eyes seem immense as they move slowly from wall to wall, trying perhaps to capture a last view of our home. Then, lifting her head, she steps out the front door.

The two soldiers are gone. A limousine is parked in front of the house, and the captain is at the wheel. We hear the creaking of doors opening and closing and hushed voices— the neighbors are watching.

The four of us fill the backseat. The major takes his place next to the captain. "Ready? ¡Vamos!" I sense a tremor that is not the car's engine but comes from right and left—I am seated between my parents.

Army cars and soldiers are at every block. They give the military salute to the major and the captain as we drive by. Ahead is the belfry of the convent chapel. I have a clear vision of the nuns on the tower balcony in their white sleeping togas. Mother Andrea, Sister Tekla, all the sisters and the young novices, the castle tower overflowing with nuns.

White togas fluttering in the moonlight. "Adios . . . adios." And as I call my farewell mentally, I don't know if it's sadness or terror that fills my eyes with tears.

We drive for a long while, accompanied by the lights of the city at either side. Then the road turns bumpy, and there are no more houses. At times we can make out pastures, huts, silhouettes of horses behind fences, rows of eucalyptus, and the shadow of a light pole thrown across the road.

At one point the major takes over the driving. While the other man sleeps, he talks to my father. "You've probably guessed where we're going, Señor Maldonado." He tells us that we are on our way to the highland, to an isolated pueblo with a military base, where a house is waiting for us. There we will be under close military surveillance. "You are among the luckier ones."

"Gracias a Dios," Mama mutters.

Papa takes out his handkerchief and blows his nose. "We'll be back," he whispers. "Maybe not as soon as we'd like, but you'll see. All this has not been in vain!" He stretches his arm across me and presses Mama's hand for a moment.

"Behind those mountains," the major says, his hand toward the horizon, which is still dark, "is all coffee land. The harvest is brought down by way of a road running through territory that is under the jurisdiction of our military base. Colonel Augusto Ferreira is in charge."

As we drive on, we feel the damp cold piercing through us. The sky is growing light. We see campesinos and donkeys along the road. Before us is a village with a small stone church and modest houses. To our right is an old fort, enclosed by a brick wall.

"That house on the hill," the major says, pointing to a whitewashed house with a tile roof, inside the wall, "that, Señor Maldonado, is your honorable prison."

回 3

I have been listening to men's voices and laughter and to the *zap-zap* of our country's flag waving in the wind. I can see the flag through a small rectangular window at the top of the wall.

Beside the army cot where I am lying, there are a night table and a straight-backed wooden chair. The tiny room has a bulb in the ceiling and a brick floor. I am covered with a sheet that feels as cold as my body. On the wall, near the cot, is an ascending line of black ants.

My parents and Ricardo are probably in rooms like this—our cells in the honorable prison? A slice of light is coming through the door, which is ajar. I delay getting up, afraid of what I may find.

The two officers left us at the door of the house with our suitcases. They seemed eager to get rid of us and drove away immediately, the major averting his eyes, saying that he would announce our arrival at the base and "Good luck, Señor Maldonado."

The door of the house was open. My father went first into the cold house, into the rooms that were still dark, Mama feeling for the light switch on the wall, muttering about blankets. By then exhaustion had set in, and I fell asleep with the singing of cocks in my ears.

Now I hear the familiar sound of Papa's cough and, after a moment, my mother's hushed voice. I sit up and put on my moccasins. I am still wearing the wool skirt and sweater in which I left the city.

Outside the room is a narrow corridor, paved with red bricks, and a sloping tile roof. It runs parallel to an equally narrow open yard, where my father sits in a white hemp hammock. He's wearing his hat and both his overcoat and poncho. On a chair near him is Mama, bundled up in her shawl.

"Here you are, Marta," he calls.

"It's ugly, isn't it?" I say, looking around the yard of packed earth where weeds grow against the brick wall that encloses the house. The wall is topped with broken bottles set in cement.

"We're together, Marta. It's something to be thankful for," Mama says.

In the center of the yard is a hole with ashes. Papa explains that the base was a hacienda once, as is the case with many military forts in small pueblos. "This house was probably the servants' quarters. They slept along that corridor on the bricks and lit a fire in this hole to warm themselves. And the rooms along the corridor, where we slept, were no doubt the foremens'."

"Where is Ricardo?"

Both point toward the room at the front of the house, next to the entrance hall. Mama is already calling it the living room.

"Papa, what happened? How did they find out about—"

"We've been talking here, your mother and I," he interrupts. "Someone at the bank obviously alerted the authorities." He is quiet for a moment and goes on, shaking his head. "I thought that withdrawing the money at the very last moment . . . It was my mistake! But, you see, I was afraid that, as has happened to others, our money would be frozen."

"You think Señor Hernández was taken to jail or something worse?"

"Marta, go find out what Ricardo is doing!" Mama orders, giving me a stern look.

The living room is large and dark, with a ceiling bulb. There are four straight-backed chairs and a round, short-legged table with two tin ashtrays.

Ricardo is standing in front of the window. He doesn't turn when I walk in, and I see he's wiping away his tears with his hand.

"It's not so bad, Ricardo." And I repeat what Mama has just said about our being together. His lips quiver, and he tries to say something but doesn't trust his voice.

I understand his disappointment. Ricardo believed all along in the success of our escape. He saw it as an adventure. While Mama and I wept when Papa told us that to leave the country was our only option, Ricardo burst out, "It's our turn to be happy again. Suffering and happiness come to people by turns. Brother Tomás said that!"

I walk to the window and stand close to him. Across the paved road through which we came is the village. We can see it clearly, the small plaza with modest, tile-roofed houses and a white stone church. One solitary tree stands in front of the only two-story house. The pueblo looks deserted; not even a dog or a donkey can be seen around the square. Below and to the left of our house, at midhill, is the base, a gray stone building with black iron Spanish-style windows and a glass-enclosed veranda. A truck and two jeeps are parked in front. There's no garden or lawn, only wild bushes and stones. To the left of the building are two rather pretty stucco houses.

A little boy, probably the child of one of the officers, is

running about. A soldier, acting as his nanny, follows behind clumsily, trying to keep up with the child.

Farther, in the direction of the city, is the green of the savanna and rows of eucalyptus, looking as remote as a postcard from a foreign land.

"Come, Ricardo, let's see the rest of the house."

He has seen it, he says, his back half turned to me.

The first room along the corridor, my parents', has two cots with a night table in between. A scratched mirror hangs on the wall. I look at my reflection. I touch my cheeks, my lips, and my hair, as if to check that all is there. I have always wanted to look like Mama and to be like my father. "Marta looks like Miguel, yet she's pretty." It's a phrase often repeated by family and friends. I have my father's light brown complexion, his high cheekbones and deep-set eyes. Every day I discover Mama's gestures and mannerisms in myself. I smile now at the mirror, somewhat surprised that nothing is changed, that I look as I did before we were taken prisoner.

The other three bedrooms along the corridor all have an army cot; a tiny, square window at the top of the wall; and ants parading the walls.

Papa and Mama are still in the yard. Heads bent toward each other, they are conversing.

"Food," she says.

"Marta and Ricardo," he answers.

After a moment Mama gets up and walks into the kitchen, a doorless area, an extension of the yard, really, but with a roof. Soot stains the wall above the primitive coal oven. A wobbly table with four aluminum coffee mugs is in a corner. "I keep thinking that perhaps there's food to be cooked, something . . . Why, there's not even a pot to heat water," she says. I walk through a door near the oven that leads to the backyard. Two man-sized wooden boxes stand there: the bathroom, a cistern with a pail; and the toilet, a wooden box with a hole over a deep hole in the ground. On the side of the corridor, midway down the hill from our house, is the base yard with the flagpole. An earth embankment separates the two yards. Several soldiers wearing ponchos dally about. One looks up, sees me, then, turning away, he mumbles something to the others and they laugh.

I scuttle back into the house. Ricardo, recovered from his tears, is in a chair near the hammock.

It's late afternoon. We are hungry and cold. We are mostly apprehensive.

My father looks up in vain for the sun, hidden behind clouds. "No wonder the natives of the Andean Mountains considered the sun their god," he says. "The catechism of the first Spanish missionaries portrayed the face of God inside the solar star." He alone has been speaking, while we listen absentmindedly. He describes the painting of a primitive artist. "A plateau covered by wheat with a thousand hands like wings floating between the golden, wheat-covered earth and the face of the sun, all embraced by the splendorous rays. That was the altiplano Indian's idea of heaven."

I am wondering about the major's words last night. Did he speak the truth when he told Papa that we were lucky and this was going to be our house imprisonment? I heard Señor Hernández telling my father about Arturo Montoya, a mutual friend, and his wife, both prisoners of the army. "She was tied up, raped, then forced to watch Arturo being shot in the head."

My mother keeps grabbing her hands, avoiding Ricardo's and my eyes. From time to time she moves her lips in prayer.

25

Suddenly we hear steps striding into the house. In front of us are an officer and a soldier.

"*Buenas tardes,*" the officer calls, touching his cap.

Mama and I rise to our feet immediately, mumbling "Good afternoon" in unison.

"Señor Maldonado!" the officer begins.

"Sit down, Margarita, Marta!" Papa interrupts.

"I am Captain Carlos Paredes. Colonel Ferreira wishes me to convey to you the rules you are to observe in this place."

He has an envelope in his hand. I notice the gun at his hip under the jacket that is half open. Although thin, the man has a belly like that of a pregnant woman. He starts reading the letter he has taken out of the envelope. "No visitors are allowed at any time. The base is the private territory of the national government. Thus any infraction will be punished by the death penalty under the martial law." The captain's high-pitched voice trembles slightly, as though he's reading a moving poem. "Colonel Ferreira asked me to emphasize this point. Any intruder slipping into the fort will be—"

"You've made yourself clear," Papa cuts in.

"All mail going or coming—"

Quack, quack. A large bird resembling a wild turkey flies over our heads, shrieking.

My father smiles, amused by the interruption, and looks up at the slow-flying bird. *Quack, quack, quack . . .* the screech goes on and fades away.

"All mail going or coming will be censored at the base," the captain shouts. "A guard will be stationed by the door of the house around the clock." He waves toward the soldier. Giving us his profile, the soldier salutes the captain and keeps turning around and around, as if moved by strings, repeating the salute, then marches outside. From the yard we hear one final clicking of his boots as he installs himself by the door of the house.

"The family of the prisoner," the captain continues, "is permitted to go to the market for an hour on Saturday mornings and to mass on Sundays, escorted by a soldier." He goes on reading to himself and nods; then, folding the letter, he places it back into the envelope. "There are other instructions. It's all here for you to read." He hands the envelope to my father, who doesn't take it at once.

"You may come down for a daily meal at the base mess hall after the officers and soldiers are through with lunch, sometime between three and four."

My father frowns. "Are there other alternatives?"

"Alternatives?" It's the captain who now looks amused.

"You mentioned that my family is allowed to go to the market."

"Yes."

"We'll take care of our meals," Papa says curtly.

"Today . . . perhaps?" I hear myself muttering.

All heads are turned toward me. Papa's eyes force my gaze down.

"We can wait until tomorrow, Marta."

"*¡Buenas tardes!*" The captain touches his cap and turns to leave.

"Captain!" Mama calls.

He turns swiftly.

"Is there a doctor around?"

"No, señora. As a matter of fact, there's not even a drug-store in the village." The man grins, rejoicing at giving us the bad news.

"But the local people, how do—"

"It's all right, Margarita!" Papa says.

27

Still smiling, the officer shrugs his shoulders. "There is a visiting army doctor, of course, for the military personnel. I am sure you understand, señora, your . . . your husband's position!"

"Good day, Captain!" Papa calls.

My mother closes her eyes briefly. We listen to the footsteps of the officer for a moment.

"No doctor, no medicines, not even a drugstore, Miguel!"

"Margarita, please. Something may come up; don't worry." Looking at me, he adds, "Soon we'll go to sleep, Marta, and you'll forget you're hungry. Tomorrow we'll compensate. Yes?" He glances from me to Ricardo.

"I'm glad you told him we won't go to their mess hall, I'm glad!" Ricardo says.

No one speaks for a while. Mama finally asks me to help her. We might as well unpack the suitcases, she says. She moves with odd energy, as if we are about to settle in for a long holiday. All the sheets we brought, she goes on, and what we need in this damp place are blankets. Then, her voice close to my ear, she adds, "The General must be pleased. Your father is providing a variation to his killing methods: this climate and without a doctor!"

4

The pueblo, which was like a ghost town yesterday, is filled with townspeople and campesinos this morning. Since an early hour the old church bells, sounding like the braying of a donkey, have been tolling. There is also the music of harmonicas and the off-pitch singing of the campesinos. *¡Fiesta!* is the one word that comes clear.

Fruits and greens, pottery and chicken, are spread all over the pavement. From the window the plaza looks like a gigantic, colorful blanket.

My mother gives us a long list. Besides the food for the week, we must also buy blankets, straw mats to cover the dampness of the brick floors, cooking pots, and insecticide for the ants.

"My name is Polo Beltrán," our escorting soldier comes in saying rather casually, skipping the military salute and the clicking of boots. He is short and stocky with a stonelike face. He is no different from the soldiers we saw everywhere in the city. "Raw recruits from the countryside or from the barrio slums," Papa often explains about the soldiers. "Some find pleasure in carrying guns and torturing and killing—they become professional instruments of terror. Others obey like robots and are helpless victims of the dictatorship."

29

To which group does Polo belong? I wonder. But my brother and I can't hide our animation as we leave the house and walk downhill.

We are eager to be a part of the festive mood of the market. Ricardo doesn't stop talking. "Are there dishes ready to eat at the market?" he wants to know. "No? What about a bakery? No bakery either?" Well, he will find the biggest banana in the plaza, he says.

There is a twitch of a smile on Polo's face. He looks at us out of the corner of his eye. One moment he seems friendly; the next, he frowns, straightening his shoulders, changing his step to a marching gait to show us that he is *la autoridad.*

"Where do you come from, Polo?" Ricardo asks.

The soldier does not answer for a moment, then says, "From around here," and his almond-shaped eyes look ahead toward the mountains in the distance, behind the church tower.

"We must move fast!" he says, emphasizing his martial pace, as we find ourselves inside the plaza, moving with the crowd. "One hour, that's what Captain Paredes orders, and then I have to report to him, and he . . ."

"He what?" I ask.

"One hour," the soldier repeats.

Everybody turns to stare at us. "Look, *los hijos del prisionero . . . nero . . . ero . . . ero*" (the prisoner's children). The whisper follows us around the square.

The campesinos chant their goods, calling every name in the diminutive. "Sweet little oranges . . . little red tomatoes . . . fresh little eggs!"

First we buy two large baskets; Ricardo takes one, I the other, and we go separate ways, Ricardo already eating the banana he had promised himself.

Trying to catch up with us, Polo steps over the tomatoes and eggs, the fruits and pottery. The peasants, not the soldier, apologize, calling him "my lieutenant." "*Perdón, mi teniente,*" an old campesina repeats, tossing away a large tomato that the soldier's boots squashed. Ricardo and I exchange a glance—we must keep close to each other and to the soldier.

Near the church a group of local men in city suits interrupt their conversation to glare at us with something more than curiosity: with condemnation of our father. My brother and I are experts at recognizing the pursed lips and flaring nostrils, the same expression we saw in our teachers and neighbors in the city.

I pretend not to notice and call a loud "Good morning!" The men half bow and glance away.

The village boys, darting their little hands to their temples in the military fashion, shout, "*¡Buenos días, Señor Alcalde, viva mi General!*"

Like an echo, our escorting soldier and other voices around us repeat, "Good morning, Mr. Mayor, long live our General!"

"*¡Buenos días, buenos días!*" a bony, spectacled man in the center of the gathering answers, lifting his hand in the manner of a priest conferring the benediction on his congregation.

Someone is doffing his hat, calling a clear, cordial "Good morning" to Ricardo and me. It's a young man standing by himself on the other side of the church. He is about twenty-five. His pale complexion makes his dark eyes intense.

"Let's keep an eye on the campesinos, Ricardo. Maybe we'll see one of Papa's friends."

My father has been an advocate of the peasants' rights in his newspaper. Often he has been criticized, even by his close friends, for his repeated editorials exposing the land-

31

owners' abuse of the campesinos. Ever since I can remember, there have been campesinos visiting our house, thanking my father for some favor. They would bring fruits, eggs, goat cheese wrapped in banana leaves, and dry herbs to make tea for my father's cough.

He would tell them about new formulas or experiments he had read about in a farmers' magazine that would improve their harvest of corn and other crops.

Often Papa would invite Ricardo and me to visit his peasant friends' huts in nearby villages. I was bored with the campesinos' rambling stories about sickness and poverty and the ghosts they saw everywhere. I had to fight my distaste to eat *mazamorra,* a dark, thick corn soup they served in gourd bowls, their thumbs immersed in the dish.

"I am a campesino, Marta," Papa would tell me. "Your grandfather lived in a hut and wore hemp sandals." And his eyes glistened with an emotion I could not share at those moments, surrounded by the toothless and rotten-toothed smiles of my father's campesinos.

Away from them, I was able to envision a hut set against a hill with the fragrance of eucalyptus and a neat little man with a poncho and hemp sandals, my grandfather, smiling at me with all his white teeth. "I am a campesino, Marta" sounded romantic in the city.

Now Ricardo and I search for a familiar face, but with their dark ponchos and battered hats, the campesinos around us all look alike. I pat the heads of the runny-nosed children, we compliment their goods, we do not haggle, but they are tight-lipped, counting our change hurriedly, trying to get rid of us, their suspicious eyes darting toward the spot where the mayor and his friends are standing. As we say good-bye, the murmur goes on, ". . . *prisionero, los hijos del prisionero.*"

"Time to go home!" the soldier announces, looking at the

loaded baskets. He's carrying the folded straw mats, a kettle, and a can of insecticide.

"I forgot something. It's very important, Polo, and I will take only a minute!" Ricardo says.

Both turn back, and I move toward the little street that leads to the paved road and up to our hill inside the fort.

The friendly young man who greeted us earlier is now standing nearby, smoking and looking bored. His rather formal black suit and tie give him the appearance of a handsome mannequin. As he sees me, he takes one step forward, coming perhaps to help me with the heavy basket, but stops abruptly and, glancing at his wristwatch, he pretends he has not seen me. The mayor and his friends, in animated conversation, are approaching.

Ricardo comes home after a short while, wearing a man-sized poncho, the same gray tone as Papa's.

"He wants to imitate Miguel in everything!" Mama comments, smiling, but I suspect that the poncho has another purpose.

"What are you hiding under the poncho, Ricardo?"

Ignoring my question, he walks away.

He shares his secret with my father. They laugh and whisper. At one point my brother, his back to me, thrusts his arms forward, Papa's hands move quickly, and there is more laughter and hissing between them. It's obvious that they are taking turns concealing under their ponchos what Ricardo brought from the market at the last moment.

I discover Papa's and Ricardo's secret: a chicken with red, shiny feathers that my brother calls Perico.

"Don't tell Mama, please, Marta. She wouldn't allow me to keep him."

At noon, while Mother and I take turns bathing, Papa and

Ricardo keep watch outside the bathroom. The soldiers sometimes climb the embankment and appear in our yard unexpectedly.

Ricardo plays hopscotch, his chicken following, oddly never moving far from Ricardo. The animal's beady eyes look around, as if surveying the surroundings.

"See, Marta? The chicken is a perfect addition to our family," my father says. "He's as distrustful of this place as we are. Why, Perico even whispers his cackling."

Indeed, the chicken keeps up a continual but low clucking. In the midst of following my brother, Perico lifts one leg and inclines his head as if to catch an unusual sound— mostly when Mama opens the squeaky door of the bathroom, alerting the three of us to fling a towel over the chicken.

⬜ 5

The sight of the deserted plaza during the week offers no variation. The dampness of the perennially gray sky seems to drip over the houses, the church, and the solitary tree that rocks in the wind. Occasionally the figure of a woman wrapped in a shawl scurries along, disappearing into the church.

The only place with activity is the cantina, a cavern near the church—it opens every day. One sees men going in, seldom coming out until six, when the cantina's owner is forced to close because of curfew. Then the men grudgingly cross the plaza on their way home, some stumbling and half falling with drunkenness. The women and children of the village are hardly seen during the week. Do they spend their lives waiting for the weekend to go to the market and to Sunday mass?

There are not many noises coming from the base during the day. Some afternoons the band plays, and the soldiers march around the flagpole while an officer grunts as if he were howling vowels, "A . . . O . . . U . . ." The band also plays rumbas and boleros, and a momentary animation fills the air. But many afternoons the only sound is that of a soldier playing intermittently on a drum, as if calling for some-

35

one who doesn't want to bother, and there is no ceremony around the flag.

During the weeks we have been here, an event takes place every Thursday at midnight. It starts with a man cursing and shouting orders. There are panting, huffing, and dragging of feet, and it's clear that the soldiers are carrying heavy loads to the trucks parked in front of the building. Often the steps come in our direction. We hear them in our backyard, hesitating one moment, advancing the next. There are also loud streams of urination. But it's the moment of stillness in between that sends a chill through us, that silence, like a precursor to their appearance in our rooms. It seems then that the doors and walls, the whole house, pants with our terror. Finally, relief: An obscenity breaks the stillness, and the command "Ready, let's go!" is followed by trucks and jeeps roaring out of the fort. At dawn we are awakened again by the growling of vehicles coming back. We listen to the men jumping down from the trucks, but there are no alarming sounds at this early hour.

"I have figured it all out," Papa said the other day. "The turmoil of Thursday nights. It's the time of week the men go to the barracks on the mountain to supervise the transportation of the coffee harvest that is brought out through the road up there. At dawn, when we hear the uproar of trucks and the men jumping, that's the arrival of the ones who were on duty the week before. That's Thursday night's agitation."

"And what about the shooting we hear sometimes during the day, what do you think happens, Miguel?" Mama asked.

He didn't know. "They probably keep up the shooting to frighten everyone around. But who knows. . . ." He didn't speak for a while. "Maybe they kill innocent people while they are up there in the barracks. Campesinos . . . they're always the victims at hand. And then they report to their commandant imaginary ambushes, tales of underground resistance. This way they keep getting promotions."

Some days the faraway shooting goes on and on. At those moments we are jumpy, Mama dropping everything. We give a start at the unexpected screeching of birds flying over our heads, and then it's a relief to laugh.

After lunch Mama and I often sit by the living room window. No sooner does the soldier who guards the door see us than he begins to pace back and forth. Rifle on his shoulder, head erect, he marches across the front of the house, stopping at each end to click his boots, his performance in our honor. Soon, however, he tires and, slumping against the wall, slips into a siesta.

At this hour the wives of Colonel Ferreira and Captain Paredes are on the base porch, drinking their after-lunch coffee. They live in the pretty stucco houses to the left of the base and take their meals at the mess hall. The child, son of the colonel, is under the permanent care of a soldier, an alert, solicitous nanny when the two women are around, but a sullen one when he's alone with the child.

In their spike heels, the two women are forever staggering on the fort's rough grounds. Always overdressed in velvet suits or flowery silk dresses with short fur jackets, they look as if they are on their way to an official reception. Sometimes, as if suddenly struck by an idea, they hurry from the porch, make a sign to their chauffeur, and, climbing into the jeep, speed out of the fort, only to return almost immediately.

My mother usually sews at this hour. Papa rests and Ricardo sketches in his room. A peaceful routine for a family under house arrest.

But there are no peaceful thoughts in my mother's mind,

nor in mine, at these moments. We hardly speak, as though we are distrustful of what we may say to each other. The air between us is a bridge where our reproaches against my father travel back and forth. Doesn't he feel responsible for our being here, constantly exposed to the whims of Colonel Ferreira and his men? Are my father's ideals more important than our safety?

Out of the corner of my eye I look at her pursed lips, the quick movement of her hand as she sews. She also looks at me covertly, at my hand scribbling in my notebook.

It occurs to me that it's in this place that I've become truly aware of my mother. Before, in our home in the city, she was a marginal presence, the color of a dress, the aroma of a perfume, an indispensable component of our surroundings that somehow did not require our attention. She was somebody to answer my brother's and my questions: "Where is Papa?" "Will we accompany him to the newspaper next Saturday?" "Will he be here for dinner?"

At the end of the day Ricardo and I were always interrupting what we were doing to check the rack in the foyer for our father's gray, rumpled hat.

How often we would see the rack loaded with hats, coats, and umbrellas, resembling a monster of many heads standing in the foyer. Then my brother and I would sit and wait, our ears alert to the voices inside my father's closed study. If there was laughter, we also laughed softly. And as the laughter grew louder, my brother's face, no doubt a reflection of my own, would take on an idiotic air, his mouth opened in a muted guffaw. It was probably Papa who was telling a joke, amusing his friends . . . on our time. If the voices got loud and the discussions were accompanied by fists pounding on the furniture, Ricardo and I would look at one another, our eyes big with alarm. But after a moment, laughter would resume and we would smile, relieved, as if we were the adults and the ones inside the study were the children reconciling.

"They're leaving now!" we would say, listening to the scraping of chairs, our eyes on the door, which remained closed. No one came out.

Upstairs Mama read and sighed—heavy sighs that would float down to us in the foyer. Ana, the maid, smoked cheroots on a chair outside the kitchen, and the dinner waited in the oven.

Some Sunday afternoons we composed our own plays with Papa—Mama our only audience. A notebook in each of our laps, we scrawled dialogue as we went along, inventing situations. They dealt with abused campesinos, judges who applied the law only to the poor, and political candidates whose merits were that they belonged to the oligarchy.

Politics bored Ricardo and me as much as it did our mother, but Papa avoided all clichés, and we doubled up with laughter at his imitations.

I recall the interrupted holidays. When Dr. Camacho prescribed a change of climate for Papa in the mountains or by the sea, we would pack for two or three weeks that never ended up being more than one week. Papa would use a phrase that he thought was humorous but that failed to make us laugh, "You see, like my pulmonary condition, our government is also chronically affected. There is a crisis, and I should be back at the newspaper."

Sighing, Mama would pack what she had so lovingly unpacked, Ricardo and I would fight with each other, and in the background Papa would make promises for another holiday. "Next time we'll go to the mountains. You'll like it there, Margarita," or "We'll go to the sea. The children love the beach," he'd say, depending on where we were, as though we had any preference, other than to enjoy an uninterrupted holiday.

"There they go!" Mama says now. Through the window I see the wives of the colonel and Captain Paredes sashaying down the steps of the base porch. The child, who has been playing about, shrieks as he sees the jeep speed out of the fort without him.

"Poor women, I bet nothing they say is taken into consideration by their husbands," I say.

"And what makes them different from me, Marta? I mean, did your father listen to me when I begged him to take that appointment he was offered in Belgium? We wouldn't be here, you know."

Although I agree with her, I protest. "How can you make comparisons, Mama, between those men and Papa!"

"I'm comparing myself with the women, Marta!"

"You've never approved of Papa's involvement in politics, have you?"

She doesn't answer my question. Lifting the sewing to her mouth, she bites the thread and sticks the needle in her blouse. "All finished, see?" She shows me the apron she has just made from a pillowcase.

"Mama, do you feel that Papa is—well, that he's selfish and thinks only about our country and the dictator, all that, and forgets about us?"

"What a thing to say, Marta! Of course I don't think such nonsense!"

"You just don't want to admit it to me, Mama. I can sense your resentment when we sit here alone."

"My resentment? What are you talking about, Marta? Why would I be resentful toward Miguel? You mean I should blame him for his attitudes about the dictator and our being here? Is that what you mean? Your father has never betrayed his beliefs. I knew what to expect from him before you were born, when I married him. I don't enjoy being here but—"

"You see? You hate it here, but you pretend you like it. When Papa is around, you walk about humming, and you cook and clean and wash, all those things you never did in our home, pretending—"

"Yes, I pretend a little in front of Miguel. Your father is ill. It would be cruel to walk about with a sullen face, to reproach him. Here he feels helpless . . . defeated." She pauses and gives me one of her piercing stares. "Marta, to encourage resentment against your father is to build future self-recrimination. One day—it's no good, Marta!"

I look away. At last I understand her silence while we sit here. She felt she could relax with me without hiding her worry about my father and our being here.

We don't speak for a while. Then she says, "Marta, do you see anyone at the market? I'm not speaking about the campesinos, of course. Do you see among the villagers any sign of sympathy toward your father, what he represents? I keep thinking of somebody who might risk taking a letter to your Uncle Alberto or to Doctor Camacho and returning with Miguel's medicines. Soon there won't be any capsules left, and without them we have nothing to control his cough." While she is saying the last phrase, her hand has been wrinkling the apron she folded a moment ago. Then quickly she smiles and begins smoothing it, as if suddenly realizing that with me, also, she needs to pretend.

⌐ 6

I have noticed two young women at the market. They are like identical twins, with dark, deep-set eyes, small, heart-shaped mouths, and a thick, glossy braid that they wrap around the head like a crown. They are pretty in an odd, spinsterish fashion. Unlike the others at the plaza, they do not stare at us.

We buy fruits from the same campesina. I smile at one of the young women and she smiles back. For a moment we are like two girls on their first day of school, eyeing each other. As I go on picking a papaya, I realize how much I miss a friend and the conversation and company that are not my parents' and my brother's. Just when I make up my mind to speak to the two women they turn their backs and are ready to leave.

"Who are they, the two señoritas?" I ask the campesina.

"The teachers," she mumbles, evasive as everyone at the plaza is with us. Then, looking at someone behind me, she bows and is all smiles. "Your sisters, Señor Profesor, they just left, the two señoritas."

The young man who resembles a handsome mannequin is approaching. I should have guessed he was their brother.

42

The three have the same appealing yet lifeless look. They remind me of the cardboard figures Papa used to cut out for Ricardo and me when we were small.

He stands by my side, and I sense his eyes on me as I go on throwing oranges into my basket. Moving closer, he asks, "How is your father?"

I don't answer for a moment. My face, no doubt, shows surprise, incredulity, mostly pleasure. Since we've been here, no one has inquired about my father. "He is all right, thank you!" I say at last. "You know about my father?"

"Is there anyone around who doesn't?" He smiles, showing his white, even teeth. "My name is Fernando." He stretches out his hand, which feels pleasantly warm as he holds mine for a moment. "We live behind the church, on the lane with the brook."

"I'm Marta Maldonado, and we live . . . well, you know where we live." Afraid that the conversation may die right there, I begin to chat away. I am also a teacher, in a way, I tell him. "I was assistant instructor to the nuns at the convent where I graduated."

"What did you teach?"

I hesitate. The extent of my teaching experience has been reading stories to first- and second-graders. "Mostly reading and vocabulary, you know."

"So you're a teacher. I'm very pleased to know that we are colleagues, you and I."

"We are, yes!" I answer in earnest.

The campesina does not take her eyes away from Fernando and me, ignoring her other customers.

"Maybe you and your brother would like to visit us and meet my mother."

"Your mother?" I ask, wondering about his sisters. "We would, yes, very much!" I can't get rid of my enthusiastic tone. I don't tell him that we are only allowed to come to the market and to mass on Sundays.

"My mother is an invalid," he says with an unexpected whine in his voice. "She's an invalid," he repeats, "and never leaves the house."

The soldier Polo, who was some steps away with Ricardo, is now watching us closely. "Look, señorita." He points to Ricardo, who is running to catch his chicken. Turning to Fernando, the soldier salutes. "See, Señor Profesor, the boy, I have to follow them both but I can't be here and there; I have only two legs."

"Ricardo!" I call, but my voice is drowned out by all the noises of the market.

"Go on; ask him to come or to wait," Fernando orders Polo.

We both look as the soldier moves away and talks to Ricardo. My brother, standing still, clutching his chicken, is beckoning to me to come. He also seems to be involved in a conversation with someone I cannot see well through the moving crowd.

"I must go. Adios, Fernando."

He walks a few steps with me, then stops. "I'll be away next week but will see you soon."

I nod and move fast to catch up with Ricardo and Polo. "We have a friend, Ricardo," I say, half panting. "And guess what, he asked about Papa!"

"Marta, here, I've been talking to—"

"*Niña* Marta, remember me?" An old campesino dressed in the light clothes and white drill poncho of the warm-climate peasantry is standing close to Ricardo, facing me. "I came to find out about—" he lowers his voice. "Is he very ill, Don Miguel?"

"He is all right!" I half shout, suddenly annoyed at the old peasant's question.

"Not so loud, señorita." He places a knobby finger on his mouth. "I am Honorio, remember?" He removes his straw hat. The wrinkled face contrasts with the black, silky hair. "You and Don Miguel have been in my humble house in Arroyo." He smiles, and I recognize his gold tooth, a sign of hierarchy among the campesinos. "The patriarch Don Honorio," they call him in Arroyo.

"I came bringing a medicine for Don Miguel." He looks around, then pulls out from under his poncho a package wrapped in a newspaper.

I take it quickly. I am disappointed to see that the medicine is a bouquet of dry herbs.

"Alfalfa and mint with parsley and sweet marjoram." He checks my face for the effect of his words, as if he is entrusting me with a treasure. "My wife Jacinta had Padre Tomás sprinkle it with holy water." He makes the sign of the cross on his chest.

"Thank you. How did you find out that we were here, Don Honorio?"

"One of the soldiers at the base, he comes from Arroyo. Pedro, the son of my neighbor Ulpiana, he sent a message. This climate is poison for Don Miguel." He rubs the fingers of one hand against his thumb, as if the air is cloth and he is testing its quality.

Ricardo has tried to distract Polo from Honorio and me, but the soldier is back near us, eyeing the bouquet. People are beginning to stare. In his light clothes, Honorio is calling attention to himself. He takes two steps backward, lifting his hat several times in the peasant manner, to bid us good-bye.

"My father will be glad to get your medicine. You came from such a distance," I whisper. He is now moving with the crowd and cannot hear me. Arroyo, a tiny village with meadows spattered with yellow daisies, is some three hours to the south of the city where we lived. To come to this highland, Honorio had to travel for days, transferring from bus to bus, walking miles. I watch his white straw hat receding, floating among the dark, battered hats of the other campesinos, then still. At the other side of the plaza, the white hat is flanked by two military caps. My heart gives a start.

"Come, Marta, we haven't finished with Mama's list," Ricardo calls me.

I do not move, my eyes fixed on the spot where Honorio's hat and the military caps have disappeared.

Two officers are waiting at the fort entrance. One is Captain Paredes, who came to our house the day we arrived. It's the other one who addresses me: "Hand me those herbs!" He snatches the bouquet from my hand and examines the herbs, turning them up and down while the captain concentrates on the newspaper in which they were wrapped. It's only at this instant that I notice the name *La Tribuna,* my father's newspaper. I stretch my hand toward the man, as if to take the paper away. It's probably an old issue Honorio has preserved, but it could be a recent one, under Hernández's direction. Did Honorio mean for Papa to see it? Does it bring good news? The captain folds the paper sloppily and tucks it under his arm. The other man is still sniffing the herbs.

"It's a peasant medicine to make tea for my father," I explain.

"One of your father's friends, disguised as a campesino, gave it to you. We know!" The officer speaks through closed lips like a ventriloquist.

"No, no," Ricardo and I repeat in unison. I add, "He's a campesino and knows nothing about my father's politics."

"Did you hear that?" The officer looks at Captain Paredes and laughs, his lips moving at last. "The friend knows nothing about her father's politics."

"What do you take us for, señorita?" Captain Paredes asks. "Did he give you anything else?"

"Nothing." And I hear myself, like the campesinos in the market, muttering, *"¡Nada, mi capitán!"*

"I watch them all the time, Captain Paredes!" Polo says, saluting and clicking his heels. I can see that he also is scared.

Ricardo is holding one of the baskets in one hand. With the other he is clasping Perico under his poncho. He looks unblinkingly from the captain to the other man.

The men are passing the bouquet between themselves, shaking it, as if they are expecting something to fall to the ground. Finally the officer drops it and gives it a kick. I start to bend, but I change my mind.

The chicken is clucking softly under Ricardo's poncho.

"What's that?" Captain Paredes asks, looking at Ricardo.

My brother's eyes grow larger.

"It's . . ." I begin.

"It's a chicken, the boy's," the soldier says, but the men are walking away.

I am looking at the bouquet on the ground, thinking of our loyal friend, wondering: Was it the newspaper or was it the dry herbs that Honorio wanted my father to have?

The captain turns and says, "And tell your father not to use you as messengers with his henchmen."

"¡Sí, mi capitán!" Ricardo and I answer.

"Your father will hear from us!" the other man says clearly in spite of his ventriloquist manner.

We are still standing in the same place, Polo also. The two men disappear at last inside the base. I can hear my heart beating. What will they do to my father, to us? Where did they take Honorio?

After a moment, Polo slaps the air with his hand, yelling, "You give me trouble, you two. Walk, move!"

At the door of the house Ricardo and I exchange a glance. We will tell our parents nothing about Honorio and the threat of the two officers.

7

Tonight, like every Saturday evening, we gather in the living room—the only room with a lock. The guffaws, singing, and clatter of bottles from the base can be heard clearly. Nothing is different, though, from other Saturday nights since we have been here. The simple, festive mood of the village's morning market turns vicious by evening at the base.

Jeeps zigzag in and out of the fort, bringing women in long, shiny dresses. From the window I watch them getting out of the jeeps, lifting their dresses to keep from stepping on them. Some wear cheap furs; others, simple coats. One is so young she is like a little girl, playing grown-up with her mother's high heels. Her long hair is loose. The others, with their pompadour hairdos, seem like giants next to the pygmy soldiers, who bustle about, helping them out of the jeeps and into the base.

"Marta, you've been at that window long enough. Come and help me with the laundry," Mama calls.

She's folding the week's laundry, muttering under her breath about the long time it takes for the clothes to dry. "Ah, this dampness! Why, the sweaters take a whole week to dry!" Complaining about the climate is my mother's way of expressing her fear on Saturday nights. She uses her hands as an iron and is smoothing a handkerchief on her thigh.

Papa is silent, as usual. Thumbs hooked in the vest under his poncho, he paces back and forth. He glances at Mama from time to time, in his eyes the helplessness I have noticed in the campesinos' eyes in the market, in Honorio's this morning. Now and then he touches Mama's shoulder, my head or Ricardo's. The sound of his steps on the bricks seems to be repeating, sor-ry, sor-ry, sor-ry.

I cannot forget the officer's threat this morning: "Your father will hear from us." Should I tell Papa? And the fantasy I often have of him writing a letter to the General comes back. In my imagination I have composed the letter: "Dear General: This is to inform you about my decision to stop my criticism of your government. I have changed my mind and would gladly accept the diplomatic position you offered me. Considerations toward my family . . ." But, as it always happens, I cannot go on with my absurd dream. My father would never write such a letter.

Ricardo is more restless than usual tonight. "I'm going to the bathroom."

"You just came back from the bathroom," Mama replies.

He is, of course, checking on Perico in his room. He imagines that the drunken soldiers will come into the house to steal his chicken.

"Ricardo!" Mama calls as he is about to sneak out. He goes to the window instead.

"The soldier has left already," Ricardo announces.

Every Saturday around midnight, when the crack of bullets begins—the men practice target shooting—the guard who is supposed to watch our door around the clock leaves to join the others. Clearly, there is no one at the base sober enough to supervise. I wonder about the colonel and his assistant. Are they also drunk? Are their wives locked in their houses as we are here?

"Sit down, Miguel; you'll cough less if you keep still," Mama says.

No sooner does Papa grab a book and sit down than we hear what we have been fearful of hearing every Saturday night: the sound of boots coming into the house.

Papa springs to his feet to seize the piece of rusty pipe that Ricardo found in the backyard. The pipe is like a spear, with a sharp point at one end. Standing by the door, Papa is no longer the frail, hunched man of every day. His face, his whole body, show determination. He will kill, if necessary, but what is the pipe against a rifle?

Mama and I are in the farthest corner of the room, holding each other, and Ricardo, in the middle, hesitates between the door and our corner.

"Get out!" Papa shouts. "Out!"

"I'm here watching over you!"

Papa scowls, and we look at one another.

"Who are you? Speak up!"

"I am your friend, Señor Don Miguel."

Slowly Mama and I begin to loosen our embrace.

"Ricardo!" Mama calls as she sees him peeking through the crack. "Get away from that door."

I'm beginning to understand; I move toward Papa.

"It's Ulpiana's son, Papa."

He looks at me for a moment. "Who? How do you know it's—"

"This morning at the market—" Ricardo starts.

"This morning we saw Ulpiana's son," I interrupt quickly, staring Ricardo into silence. I can still see Honorio's white straw hat between the two army caps.

"Go on, Papa, ask him if he's Ulpiana's son." I speak loudly.

"*Sí,* I am Pedro."

But my father is still doubtful. After a moment we hear

the soldier's steps retreating. "Wait!" Papa lifts the door's latch.

Rifle on his shoulder, chest thrown out, the soldier wants to show us that he is our protector.

My father's face breaks into a grin. "Pedro, of course it's you. Last time I was in Arroyo, you were a boy like my son here and going to school." His arms are around the soldier.

"¡Sí, Señor Don Miguel!"

Papa inquires about Ulpiana and each one of Pedro's brothers and sisters, recalling the names and afflictions of each one of them. "I had no opportunity to go back and find out about the land. Señor Arrieta promised me you were to continue living there. Is it all right?"

"No one pesters us now. You fixed it for us, Señor Don Miguel." Pedro's eyes do not leave Papa. I have seen this expression before, in our visits to the huts. The peasants surrounding Papa, repeating, "Sí, Señor Don Miguel," as if his name is a prayer that will make miracles.

His godfather, Don Honorio, came all the way from Arroyo to ask him to keep an eye on Don Miguel and his family, the soldier is saying. "I promised my padrino I'll watch over you."

"You mean Honorio was here?"

"Yesterday, but he left this morning."

I want to ask, Are you sure Honorio got away all right?

"But isn't it dangerous for you to come on your own to stand by our door, Pedro?"

"No, señor. Saturday night they're all locos over there"—he waves toward the base—"crazies, even the big chief, the colonel."

My father turns suddenly serious. "I don't know. . . . Honorio shouldn't have come!"

Ricardo and I look at each other.

"Many know Honorio. He's a leader among the campesinos, and everyone knows he's my friend."

"He sure is your friend, Señor Don Miguel."

Papa turns to Mama, then to Ricardo and me. "We're lucky to have friends like Honorio and Pedro. Better go back to the door now, Pedrito. Thank you!"

"*Gracias, gracias,*" we repeat.

The soldier smiles, his eyes still on Papa, then moves away.

We close the door softly and return to our chairs. My father's lips quiver for a moment, but he says nothing. He is touched by Honorio's and Pedro's gesture.

"Your friends, the campesinos, Miguel, they're our true friends. One day, I hope, we can do something for Pedro," Mama says.

Winking at Papa, Ricardo says, "When we go back to the city, would you have Pedro at our home for dinner, Mama?"

We often tease Mama, accusing her of being a snob like her brother, Uncle Alberto.

"That's a silly question, Ricardo. I'm thinking of something more substantial, like—"

"Like introducing Pedrito to Uncle Alberto and his daughter Lucía?"

"Don't tease me, Miguel," she says, smiling. We all smile, enjoying the protection of our friend Pedro.

8

For the convenience of Colonel Ferreira and his men, who sleep off their hangovers all Sunday morning, a priest comes from a nearby pueblo to celebrate mass at noon.

Going to church is Mama's only outing. "I wish there would be an early mass instead of this twelve o'clock circus!" she complains.

To avoid crossing the plaza where peasants, children, and dogs dash about, excited by the fireworks that begin at an early hour, Polo guides us along a trail that circles the village. It's a picturesque path with a stream. Alongside the path there are wooden crosses adorned with faded paper carnations and roses. Townspeople and campesinos from the area bury their dead at random there, although there's a cemetery to the north of the village.

The names of the deceased are clumsily written on the wooden crosses. One cross stands out: HERE LIE THE REMAINS OF FULGENCIO SEPÚLVEDA, A GOOD HUSBAND AND FATHER, PUNISHED WITH A BULLET BY THE MIGHTY HAND OF OUR MAYOR.

We enter the church through the back door and sit on the backless benches with the campesinos. The benches to the right of the altar are for the army men and the villagers.

All the beautifying of the church has gone into the pulpit,

a white-painted box with engraved golden baby angels. It hangs like a cage from the dusty beams.

On either side of the crucifix, in the center of the altar, are two chipped, life-size statues: Saint Anthony with a missing arm and an unknown saint clothed in rags, a beggar saint, stretching one hand to receive charity and half lifting one knee to display a sore. It's in front of this saint that the campesinos crowd to drop coins and light candles.

"What's the name of the beggar saint?" we asked Polo the first day we came to church.

"*El Santico,*" answered the soldier.

Although the mass is scheduled for twelve, it starts only when the army men, in procession, enter the church, usually at one o'clock. An officer, carrying the national flag with a picture of the General attached to the flag, comes in first. He goes up to the altar and stands at one side, facing the people. Then comes the band, playing a march. Colonel Ferreira, wearing dark glasses, and Captain Paredes, both men holding their wives' arms, follow. The two women's dresses shine like the dresses of the prostitutes the night before. Behind them marches the skinny mayor, contrasting with his fat wife, who presses against her bosom a black fur, like a cat, and at the tail end, the officers and the soldiers.

The stamping procession brings the frightened peasants to their knees. Some campesinas lift their babies, as if offering them to the colonel.

Fernando and his sisters, both wearing black veils like widows, sit on the bench close to the main entrance. I'm glad they are far away from us.

Each Sunday Mama participates in what she calls the circus. In church she gives full rein to the anguish she restrains during the week. Lips quivering, eyes lifted up to the ceiling, her face is a mixture of ardor and despair that makes heads turn. "The poor thing, *la señora, pobrecita.*" Ricardo and I can hear the hissing of the campesinos while lowering our eyes with embarrassment. "We must talk to Mama, really!" we mutter, but we never say a word.

It is, perhaps, also for the convenience of Colonel Ferreira, who stifles yawns all throughout the mass, that the priest is robbed every Sunday of the opportunity to climb the golden cage to preach.

The highlight of Sunday mass is the Elevation. At that moment, braying bells, fireworks, barking dogs, and the band playing the national anthem explode while the campesinos howl in chorus, *"Perdón, Señor, perdón,"* striking their breasts, and the terrified children squeal.

Mama shakes her head, and my brother and I bite our lips to keep from laughing. After the Elevation, the campesinos, as well as the army men and the villagers, begin to leave, although the mass is still going on.

On Sundays Papa does not type. He waits for us in the front yard with a book.

"How was the circus, Margarita?"

He is cheerful, or rather he makes an effort to appear cheerful. "We must start," he says, pointing to the three chairs around the hammock. Sunday is English-lesson day. He opens the book, *Cortizos' Easy Guide to Learning English.* "We don't need a teacher," he repeats every Sunday. "You see the text has an articulation system based on Spanish equivalents that guarantees a perfect pronunciation. 'Welcome, Meester González, you arr in a free country now.'" (A Mr. González, no doubt a political exile, is the subject of the conversation lessons.) " 'Speek with no fear, Meester González!' "

56

He acts out the lessons as he moves about the yard. Bowing extravagantly in front of Mama, pulling his reading glasses down his nose, skipping from one spot to another, he asks questions of Ricardo and me. But his clowning, which used to make us laugh, brings only forced smiles from my brother and me and from Mama, who says, "Be still, Miguel, or you'll have a fit of coughing."

He pretends not to notice our long faces, which even Mama doesn't bother to conceal on Sundays—Sundays are the beginning of another interminable week.

"It's your turn, Margarita!"

"Please, Miguel, leave me out of this. I'm too old to learn English."

"Come, dear. Speek with no fear, Señora Margarita!"

Mama sighs and repeats with a pronunciation that sounds better than his and that he corrects, "Again, speek, speek, see?"

He points at things in the yard so that we can identify them in English.

"Weeds."

"Wall."

"Ashes."

His emphasis, however, is on Señor González's phrases, which he repeats over and over. "Welcome . . . you arr in a free country now!"

Today, as soon as the lesson is finished, Ricardo disappears into his room. After a moment Mama calls, "Ricardo, will you come out of that room with your silly chicken!"

I turn to Papa, now relaxing in the hammock. "Does Mama know about Perico?"

"Of course I know. The three of you seem to believe that I'm blind, deaf, and dumb. Who do you suppose has been cleaning the chicken droppings that are everywhere?"

Ricardo is at the door of his room, clutching his pet, glancing at Mama. "You don't mind my having Perico? I'll clean up after him, I promise, Mama."

"You must find a place for the animal besides your room. And no more whistling, Ricardo. I'd rather hear the chicken's clucking."

We laugh.

"Well, the mystery is over," Papa says. "We'll have to think of something else, Ricardo. Your mother is too clever!"

"Mama, I want to show you the tricks I've taught Perico," Ricardo says, putting the chicken on the ground, dashing into his room to get the sticks and miniature fences he has made for his chicken's act.

Mama sighs.

Papa chuckles.

Because of being constantly in hiding, the chicken moves slowly, with comical solemnity.

Papa gets up from the hammock.

"Welcome, Perico, you arr in a free country now!" He bows.

9

My father types at all hours, his index fingers pounding steadily at the Remington. One moment he nods; the next, he rips the paper out of the typewriter to toss it in the garbage pail. From time to time he leafs through a notebook he carries in his vest pocket.

Paper for typing is his one order to my brother and to me when we go to the market. We buy lined school notebooks, the only paper available in the village's one store. Ricardo tears away the cover with the picture of the General and arranges the sheets in stacks.

Mama has made improvements around the house. The scratched tops of the night tables are now covered with linen napkins, and the fourth bedroom, at the end of the corridor, is the linen room. There, in wooden boxes that are used as tables or drawers, she has arranged the bed linens and our clothes.

Ricardo is the provider of our "tables." He finds them in a pile at the back of the base building, where the soldiers discard the wooden cases, empty of their whiskey and American canned foods. At siesta hour, when everyone at the base is indoors, my brother walks downhill to explore. At first Mama objected. Were we now like the beggars of our city, digging into garbage cans? But she has made use of all his findings.

We have learned to speak, even to argue, in low voices. Hearing ourselves reminds me of the convent—the monotonous murmur of the nuns saying the rosary. But the sound of my father's cough is almost as persistent as his typing.

"Mama, give him one of those capsules that stop his cough, please!" Ricardo says, placing his hands over his ears.

"I'm saving the capsules. I know what you're thinking: to save medicines! But you see, we don't know how long we'll be here."

She leaves her chair to walk to the wall topped with the broken bottles. She bends to the ground. "Look, the weeds have tiny purple flowers. See? I have a notion to plant them in a pot."

Every day Mama discovers something new. She acts like the hostess of a pension, pointing out to us the advantages of this place, which she alone sees.

At last Papa comes out, a few typed pages in his hand. He approaches, smiling, winking at Ricardo with the air of someone who is bringing good news.

"We mustn't despair. This cannot last much longer," he says. "We'll be back in our home soon, you'll see."

"You think so, Papa, really?" Ricardo asks.

I pretend to be absorbed in my reading. I find it difficult to concentrate on *Don Quixote,* but more difficult to listen to Papa's promises. "It won't last much longer," he also repeated for months in the city. I have no faith in his predictions, yet I feel disloyal for not believing my father.

"But, Miguel, we have no idea of what's going on. Why are you so optimistic?"

"True, Margarita, we don't read or hear news, but one

can judge, considering the situation we left in the city."

Mama and I glance at each other. We have spoken about the official newspaper that one of the soldiers leaves every day by the front door. Mama and I would like to read it, but to bring it into the house is an insult to Papa. It's something more. Not touching the papers that pile up day after day by the door of the house is our one gesture of pride. The soldier who guards the door is forever picking up the newspaper pages that the wind scatters downhill.

"How much longer do you think we'll be here, Papa?"

"Maybe, as your mother thinks, Ricardo, I'm being an optimist; I really think that soon we'll hear something."

"I wish he would be killed, the General!"

"What we want is to free the country of him."

"And then we'll go back to the city and your newspaper will be like before and everything again—"

"And you'll go back to school, Ricardo!" Mama interrupts.

"Everything will again be as before, yes, Ricardo." Papa grows animated answering questions. He begins coughing.

My brother jumps up to bring him a glass of water. Papa gestures "no" with his hand and, while coughing, keeps motioning to Ricardo to sit down. "It's all right," he says finally.

After a moment Papa says, "I daresay the downfall of the tyrant is near. We'll hear that he either sought refuge in an embassy or, most probably, that he escaped in one of the air force planes."

I try not to listen, but at the same time I want to hear. My father's words and the words I am reading jumble in my head.

". . . friends will come. . . . Uncle Alberto and your mother's relatives will also be here. They'll come to drive us back to the city."

"But do they know where we are, Papa?"

"This is not such a big country, Ricardo. Somehow one manages to find out about these things."

"But if they know, why hasn't anyone tried to help us?"

"It's better not to dwell on this. Don't forget, Ricardo, that it's their lives they are risking by getting in touch with us." For a moment no one speaks; then Papa goes on. "There will be much talking and praising, of course. Everyone will steal a moment to say his short speech. It will all be a little ridiculous and tiresome, especially for your mother, but we'll survive our small glory, won't we, Margarita?"

"Bravo!"

"Hush, Ricardo!" Mama says.

Papa chuckles.

"Marta, I want you to hear something I typed this afternoon."

While he's shuffling the pages and before he starts reading, I am guessing what's coming: *justice, liberty, free press*—words that have lost their meaning. I have heard about our country and the dictator to satiation. The subject has become as arid as the pit of ashes in the little yard.

Papa reads: " 'Arrests were being made by the hundreds. . . . U.S. technical advisors . . . police intelligence . . . money lavished . . . as though the Treasury is bottomless.' "

I make an effort to concentrate, but my attention escapes before the conclusion of each phrase.

" '. . . have joined the opposition abroad.' "

I swing my foot; I touch my hair. The voice of my father falls heavily, a chain tying me to the chair.

"Words!" I hear myself say. "What's the point of all this, Papa? I mean, who's going to read it except us?"

There's silence while he regards me for a moment. I don't need to look at Mama's and Ricardo's faces turned toward me; I feel their disapproval.

"I understand your impatience, Marta. Words indeed. It's hard to avoid them. In my daily typing I recount events simply. Nicolás Julián, for instance, gunned down because he kept broadcasting the names of missing persons; Fabio Sierra, editor of the university magazine—his crime was to write about the campesinos and students who were garrotted and dumped in a ravine after demonstrating against the regime. Fabio was executed in front of his parents and sisters. Short case histories, that's what my typing is all about: José Lopez, Alicia Rojas, Guillermo Rico, María Elena Becerra . . . the list is endless. Facts alone. I refrain from commenting. I'm also tired of words! What's the point, you ask, who's going to read all this? Good question. Should I be silent, Marta?" He shakes his head. "I intend to go on while I have strength," he continues. "You see, Marta, I happen to believe that every individual, no matter how insignificant, has a responsibility for the events of his time."

"You want Papa to be like Uncle Alberto?" Ricardo asks.

"It's a matter of choice, Ricardo," Papa says.

"It's a matter of conscience, Miguel." Mama approaches with a cup of consommé. "Here, Miguel, take a sip."

"Were you reading about Don José and all those people, Papa? I didn't understand."

"You weren't listening. I was reading a synopsis of the situation up to the day we left the city, what the censored press couldn't publish and what I learned from reliable sources." He takes one page and reads:

" 'On August 16th, Colonel Enrique Oviedo, revolted by the cruelties of the regime, fled the country. He has joined the opposition abroad against the dictator.

" 'A pastoral letter condemning the everyday crimes and disappearances was being prepared by the Pope's ambassador.

" 'Minor defections in the armed forces . . .' Well, no

need to go on. A person linked to the government called me two days before the night we were apprehended. 'Don't quote me, Miguel, but panic has seized the government,' he told me, but who knows. . . . Maybe I'm suffering from one of my delusions."

"Your predictions are usually right, Miguel. I'm glad you read it aloud. Here." Mama has been offering him a spoon of consommé.

"May I read it, Papa? I'd like to," Ricardo asks.

"I'm sorry," I mumble. "I don't know, it's just that sometimes I can't concentrate." Tears sting my eyes. Quickly I rise to go to my room.

▣ 10

What a relief to see Polo waiting for us by the door—last week he was on duty. The bowlegged soldier who escorted us to the market had one word for us, *"¡Arre!"* the term used for mules and donkeys. On our way back he didn't help us with the heavy baskets. At one point we paused to rest on the hill, and he jabbed Ricardo with his rifle, saying, *"¡Arre! ¡Arre!"* I turned sharply, to find his small, slanted eyes fixed on my dress. He went on jabbing Ricardo with the rifle, snickering, while my brother kept falling and cursing the soldier under his breath.

"Stop it!" I finally said. "We'll report you to the colonel!"

Somehow the threat worked. He walked away, and we climbed the last steps uphill by ourselves. Ricardo was teary-eyed, biting his lips, but he composed himself before we entered the house.

Papa's description of the soldiers came to mind: "Some become instruments of terror."

"Good morning, Polo," we greet the soldier. The guard stationed by the door of the house stands at attention as usual.

"¡Vamos!" Polo says, and the three of us rush downhill together. The sun is out today, there's a soft breeze, and

we feel the thrill of being out, away from Papa's cough.

"Where is the chicken this morning?" Polo inquires.

Ricardo says he won't have to hide him anymore. "Mama knows about Perico."

"She didn't before? Sure she did! Chickens stink!"

We laugh.

I see Fernando at the bottom of the hill by the fort wall. He paces back and forth, looking up, waiting for us.

He touches his hat to greet me and comes over. "I've been thinking about what you said the other day, Marta," he begins immediately, "that you have teaching experience. My sisters and I, we were talking." I have the feeling that he has rehearsed what he's saying. "There are too many children, you see. I'm sure that Colonel Ferreira will want to take advantage of your being here. He knows we need help."

My brother walks ahead quickly. Polo can't make up his mind. One moment he is ahead with Ricardo; the next, near Fernando and me, listening to our conversation.

"I can't promise anything, but I see no reason why you couldn't come and teach. All this, of course, if you're interested, Marta."

I feel anticipation. To be out of the house every day and with Fernando and his sisters, people my own age, is the most appealing prospect I have had in months.

"I'm sure that writing a note to Colonel Ferreira, explaining that you're a teacher . . ." Fernando is saying.

"I'd like it very much, but my father . . . He'll say no, Fernando."

Polo has dashed ahead to Ricardo. They are standing at the corner of the little street that leads to the plaza.

"And your sisters, do they agree with this?"

"Cecilia is delighted and Elisa, well, she knows we need

somebody else." Then he says, "It's a matter of convincing my mother and the colonel."

"You haven't met my brother, have you, Fernando?" I say as we reach the corner.

"¡Hola!" Fernando stretches out his hand, but Ricardo, bowing slightly, is already walking away.

"Wait, Ricardo. I want to tell you something. Fernando is inviting me to teach in—"

"Polo just told me. Papa will say no," he calls over his shoulder.

We are in the market crowd. As usual, heads turn toward us. But today there is a trace of a smile on the campesinos' faces. The presence of the Señor Profesor, as they call Fernando, close to me, suddenly makes me acceptable. A boy rushes up and gives Fernando a tangerine. Fernando explains that it's one of his pupils.

Ricardo and the soldier are off by themselves.

The chatting of the villagers and the cries of the campesinos offering their goods make it impossible to carry on a conversation as we go on strolling.

"Señorita, come!" a campesina calls me, lifting a papaya. "Here, I'll give you a good price!" For the first time I am being addressed as though I were one of the villagers.

"Good morning, Señor Profesor," they call from right and left.

He peels the tangerine, offering me half. I like Fernando, that he walks by my side unconcerned about the stares of the townspeople and the campesinos.

"I don't see your sisters this morning," I shout over the noise.

"They . . . my mother"—then close to my ear, he repeats—"They are with my mother. We don't like to leave her alone."

"And your father?"

"It's too noisy here. Come, let's go." He takes my arm and guides me toward the church.

"But Ricardo, I mustn't leave him," I say, touching Mama's list in my cardigan pocket. "I should start shopping."

"Just for a moment, Marta."

We climb the stone steps to the paved terrace that surrounds the church and walk to the back. With his handkerchief, Fernando cleans a place for us to sit.

We're facing a dirt road descending to the valley. A campesino between two donkeys moves downhill slowly. No one else is about.

"Aren't you taking a risk to be seen with me?"

"Everybody at the market saw us already!" He laughs.

"But here with me alone?" I'm thinking of his family. "Your house is somewhere around here, no?"

He nods, pointing vaguely in the direction of a red roof half visible under a large mahogany tree.

"I was asking about your father," Marta says.

He pulls out a package of cigarettes and offers me one. I say I don't smoke.

"He doesn't live here. Cecilia was a baby when he abandoned us."

"I'm sorry."

"Don't be! I have no feelings whatsoever for my father." He fishes for the matches. "He could be in the plaza right now and I wouldn't recognize him. He's a stranger to me." He makes a noise like a chuckle, but he isn't laughing. "My father burdened me with responsibility that was his, you see. I have to look after my mother and sisters." He inhales the cigarette.

I don't know what to say. I wish I hadn't asked about his father. Fernando seems different from a moment ago when

68

we were at the plaza. He is unappealing in his resentment—
or is it sadness?

"Where is Fernando?"

"Uh?"

"My friend who brought me here, you know, the Señor
Profesor."

He laughs.

"Yes, that's it, I'm stuck in this pueblo, 'the Señor Profesor,' 'the man of the family,' and 'the mayor's nephew,' my
three credentials. Impressive, no?"

"You are the mayor's—you mean the mayor is your uncle?"

Fernando appears not to be listening. "I used to like it
when I was a boy to hear people calling me the *hombre de
la familia.*"

"Had I known that he was your uncle—I shouldn't be
here with you."

Fernando either pretends not to hear or is too absorbed in
what he's saying.

"To go to the Universidad Nacional and be an engi-
neer, that was what I wanted, but there was no money, of
course."

"Is he your father's brother?"

"My mother's older brother, Marta." He acknowledges
my question at last, dropping the cigarette, squashing and
grinding it with his heel.

I must not be here with the mayor's nephew, I'm saying
to myself, but then immediately I think: If I am to have my
father's approval for every friend I pick, only the campesinos would be my friends in this place.

"My mother keeps telling me I could have a career, like
my uncle. She means I could turn myself into a local politician,
climbing on a platform to scream lies and empty phrases,
picking out a winner among the candidates who come to

this pueblo at election time and cheating for him—the whole mess. I'm sorry, Marta, I didn't mean to rant against politicians. I know that your father—I didn't mean . . .''

"My father? I don't understand.''

"He's a politician, isn't he?''

"So that's what you think my father is, someone like your mayor uncle? You don't know a damn thing about my father! He's struggled all his life against the oligarchy and the corruption of government. Why do you think he's here?'' My voice is quivering.

"Marta!'' He tries to grab my hand. I take it away quickly.

"If Papa were an opportunist, we wouldn't be here; we would be in Europe, where the General wanted to send us so that my father's newspaper would stop condemning his actions!''

"Shhh!'' He looks around.

For the first time I am saying what so many times I have wanted to shout to the nuns and to my classmates but have never dared.

"I apologize, Marta. I made a mistake and I had no intention, either, of going on about myself.''

"It's getting late!''

"Sit down, Marta.'' He pulls me down by the arm.

I sit, and we say nothing while he takes time to light a cigarette.

"Knowing you made me realize about my life in this pueblo . . . my life! It's as if before, my world was an alley and now suddenly I see a panorama. It's because of you, Marta.''

"I'm glad it's my fault, I mean the panorama instead of the alley.''

"I suppose that for you I must be a backward villager, a campesino.''

"You're the mayor's nephew,'' I mumble to myself.

"What's that?''

"Nothing."

A gust of wind threatens his hat, and he takes it off. He is more handsome without the black felt hat. His curly hair blows in the wind. I look at his dark suit, the starched white shirt and tie, wondering if he dresses like an old man to look his part as *"el hombre de la familia,"* the man of the family.

If something happens to my father here, would Ricardo also feel like Fernando, condemned to—I rub my head, as if to reject the thought about Papa.

"Ricardo is probably wondering about me."

"He doesn't like me, your little brother."

"He doesn't like anyone at this point. That's why he got himself a chicken, to turn his mind away from the rest."

All of a sudden I begin telling Fernando about Honorio. ". . . and then he was with two military men, leaving the market. I'm afraid that something happened to him, Fernando. What do you think?"

I wait for his answer, longing to hear a word of reassurance.

"I hate this pueblo, Marta!" he says after a while.

"They went that way, my father's friend and the two army men." I point to my right. "Where would that lead, Fernando? Is that the road that goes up to the barracks in the mountains where they go every week?"

"Who?"

"The men from the base, you know. Isn't that where they take turns spending a week?"

"And you haven't seen the worst in this pueblo yet—the rainy season!"

"Your uncle probably knows what happened to old Honorio!"

Fernando reacts at last. "I don't know what my uncle knows, Marta. When I talk to him, which isn't often, I don't ask questions that are not my business." He looks at me intently. "My uncle is not a military man, you must know. For political convenience, the army didn't impose a military mayor here, as they have in most pueblos. You see, the nearby landowners and the townspeople support my uncle. They've known him for years, but he, my uncle, has to be cautious. He has to go along with the army, you understand."

"I understand that it's a matter of choice. Your uncle obviously has chosen to cooperate with the dictator."

"What else can he do? If he doesn't—listen, Marta, you don't understand. My uncle knows what to do. He's been the mayor of this village for more years than I can remember. It's not easy, his position, you know."

"I must go, really!" I am already on my feet.

"Wait, Marta! Why are we talking all this nonsense? You haven't even said if you are coming to teach."

"It's impossible, really, Fernando. We both know it."

"Maybe, but I want to try. Do you authorize me to send a note to Colonel Ferreira, yes?"

To my surprise I hear myself saying, "Can I meet your mother and sisters first?"

"Of course. What about next Saturday? Will you come for a visit?"

"It'll have to be a very short one."

"That's all right. I'll wait by the wall of the fort like today." He presses my hand. "Marta—" he begins.

"Let's go. My brother and the soldier. We've been here too long. I also worry about you in the company of *la hija del prisionero.*'"

"'*El Señor Profesor* and *la hija del prisionero,*' romantic, no?"

"Dangerous, Fernando!"

We walk toward the front of the church, back to the noise of the market.

I search for my brother's light brown hair, his head, which stands a few inches taller than those of the villagers and campesinos. I can't see him. Has he left, and is he telling Mama that I disappeared? "Oh, God, where is he?" I say in panic.

"Don't get excited, Marta." We are both standing on the steps below the terrace, from where we can survey the plaza crowd better. Fernando spots them. "There, see? There they are!" He waves. "They have seen us already."

Ricardo advances, gesturing. "Are you crazy?" he yells, and heads turn from him to us on the steps. "Where were you? You . . . !"

"You give me headaches, señorita. I was about to go report you missing."

Fernando pats the soldier's shoulder, explaining that we were right there all the time. "Everything is all right!" Polo smiles, subdued. Ricardo turns away.

"Good-bye, Marta, Ricardo." Fernando lowers his voice. "Next Saturday, don't forget, Marta."

There are only bananas and a papaya in the basket the soldier is carrying and in Ricardo's, a bag of corn for Perico.

"He's a spy, your stupid friend."

"You've read too many comic books, Ricardo."

"The Señor Profesor and the mayor, they are the most important people around here," Polo says.

"Sure, 'the mighty mayor,' we know. I've seen the cross in the cemetery, haven't you, Marta?"

"The cemetery?" I have forgotten.

Ricardo whispers, " 'Here lie the remains of Fulgencio Sepúlveda, a good husband and father, punished with a bullet by the mighty hand of our mayor.' "

"Shut up, Ricardo!"

With Mama's list in my hand, I move about quickly to buy the weekly supplies.

⊡ 11

There has always been a fifth presence, an intruder in our family, the "tyrant" against whom my father neglected to fight. Doctor Camacho has given it different names: chronic lung congestion, severe bronchial debilitation, and lesion of the pulmonary cells.

The names were given to us to choose, as when an old friend of the family who performs clever tricks displays a handful of cards, saying, "Pick one!" Chronic lung congestion was my choice. I think of the times I have repeated it foolishly, filling my mouth with the words as if I were mentioning an honor bestowed upon my father. Ricardo calls it simply Papa's cough, and Mama, who dislikes lies and big words, refers to it as Miguel's illness.

We are in the living room, and my father is in his room resting. My mother is giving us a new regulation. We are not supposed to get too close to our father and should not give him a good-night kiss. She explains that this morning she placed the chairs in the yard differently. Although still to the right and to the left of the hammock, my brother's and my chairs are at a distance. "So that when your father coughs, you are not exposed."

She speaks quickly, moving about the room with a rag in

her hand, dusting. Usually when she speaks of Papa's health, she lowers her voice, almost to a whisper.

"But Papa's cough is nothing new."

"What's new, Ricardo, is that here we don't have a doctor to control his illness. And you know what he has is contagious." He himself told her last night that he would be more comfortable alone in the bedroom, she adds.

"And where will you sleep?" We both want to know.

"I don't know what I'll do—maybe I'll put my cot in the linen room. It makes him more restless to keep me awake at night when he coughs." She keeps flicking the rag against a chair.

"Is it very serious with him, Mama?" Ricardo's eyes are pleading for comfort rather than for the truth.

She answers after a moment. "We mustn't despair. Maybe, as your father says, we'll be in our own home soon."

There was another time—we were small then—when Mama ordered us not to be near Papa because he had a "sore throat." We were spending some time in a cottage on the mountain. I can still see my father in a rocking chair on the porch and Ricardo and me, away from him in a corner, while he cut out cardboard figures for us. We watched the sombreros and donkeys, the stars and rabbits, springing from his hands as if he were a magician. We collected the figures in a tin box. One morning, the day before we were to return to the city, Mama took my brother and me for a walk up the mountain. To our surprise, she pulled our tin box with the figures out of her coat pocket. "We must set them free before we leave," she said and began tossing them one by one down the mountain. Ricardo cried as he watched his rabbits and donkeys flying, disappearing. "But you see, dear, the city air is not healthy for them," Mama said. I understood, for the first time, that she was speaking of contamination and that it was from more than a sore throat that Papa suffered.

"Sit down, Mama, please," Ricardo calls now. She is in the corner, dusting the typewriter and books. "I have an idea, Mama. I can go to the city Saturday night while the men at the base are drunk. It'll be easy to sneak out of the fort at midnight and Pedrito, he'll help us. Wait, Mama, let me finish, wait!"

My mother has been shaking her head, motioning for him to stop.

"I'll go to Doctor Camacho, get medicine for Papa, and then the next Saturday I'll return when the men at the base—"

"Enough, Ricardo! You're speaking nonsense. How am I supposed to explain your absence to your father, and where would you go in the city if you ever got there alive? To Alberto's house? I can see your uncle . . . frantic, debating if perhaps he should call the authorities and wondering whose idea it was to risk his safety and his family's. Let's be sensible, Ricardo."

"But we must try to do something!" I say.

Her lips narrow into a tight-mouthed smile, a new gesture she has acquired since we have been here, as if to tell us, "You children don't understand; you simply don't understand!"

After a moment Ricardo looks at me and moves his lips silently, pronouncing "Fer-nan-do."

My friend indeed! Will he be able to help us? I wonder. I'm lucky to have a friend. Fernando alone takes my mind away from my father's illness.

All this week I have been thinking what to wear to visit Fernando's family, as though I have a choice. Two skirts, a jumper, a cardigan, my favorite red dress with bows, and four blouses, that's my wardrobe. The blouses used to be white but have turned gray from washing with ordinary soap and cold water. My cardigan is also the color of lead. When we were getting ready to leave the country, I was smuggling clothes into my suitcase. Mama would take them out. "We must keep our luggage light," she would say. "You'll get some new clothes, Marta; we'll be in a lovely city."

"Quito? Lima? Buenos Aires?" Ricardo and I wanted to know.

"San José de Costa Rica," Mama told us only the other day. A country where there is no repression and under a leader my father much admires.

Now Mama looks at the red ribbon I have tied around my head, but she says what she repeats every Saturday as we are leaving the house, "Don't forget the aspirins and alcohol." Alcohol and aspirins are the only available medicines in the village store.

Ricardo greets my friend cordially. And Fernando inquires if he is also coming to visit his family.

"I'd like to, but I'll do the shopping to save time."

Today he doesn't walk ahead, but I sense his effort to be friendly. Pleased with my brother's manner, Fernando addresses all his remarks to Ricardo. The singing of the campesinos and the harmonicas, aren't they a nuisance so early in the morning? And the bells. "We're so close to the church we hear them as if they're clanging on our roof," Fernando says, and Ricardo laughs.

Sensing that something is different, Polo scowls with suspicion. "Where are you going, señorita?" he asks me, looking at the red ribbon in my hair. "What you did last week was no good. Remember Captain Paredes and Teniente Rosado that morning they took the herbs away? You better stay close to your brother and me."

Fernando, who is talking to Ricardo but listening to Polo,

answers, "I'll take responsibility. She's going with me for a short while, Polo, to visit my family."

"But I don't want trouble."

"You see, my mother wishes to meet Señorita Marta, and she can't get out; she's an invalid."

"Yes, la señora, the poor thing, but . . ."

"We'll meet you by the church, Polo." Fernando puts his hand on the soldier's back. The magic touch of the Señor Profesor turns Polo agreeable immediately. "All right," he says. "A short visit, please!"

"Marta!" Ricardo suddenly turns to call me. Although he says nothing, I read the message in his eyes clearly: Don't forget, ask him to help us, get him to do something for Papa. "Have a good visit!" he says after a moment.

Fernando takes my elbow, and we leave them.

⌘ 12

To avoid the corner where his uncle and the locals who surround him gather every Saturday, Fernando leads me to the opposite side of the plaza.

"Polo says that you and your uncle are the most important people in this pueblo."

He smiles. "To the campesinos and the soldiers, my uncle is a big man. They think he owns the pueblo."

"He probably disapproves of our friendship."

"I don't care. He doesn't own me, you know." He frowns and for a while says nothing.

We are on the lane behind the church, approaching a white wooden house with a balcony porch, a pretty house with a huge tree hovering over it. I have the momentary feeling that I am somewhere else. A radio is playing full volume. I recognize the official broadcast, "La Voz de la Nación." Behind the announcer's voice, a band is playing a march.

We go up a few steps onto the porch, and it's only now I realize that the sound of the radio is coming from inside the house. The first thing I notice in the front room is a large picture of the General.

"This is the main classroom," Fernando explains. There

79

are several rows of backless benches. "We live at the back of the house."

I smell soiled hemp sandals and garlic—the smell of the campesinos that clings also to the churches in the city. On the wall are newspaper pictures of the General presiding at various official and religious functions.

I follow Fernando out to the veranda, hardly hearing what he's saying, but he seems unperturbed by the music and shouting coming from the radio.

"An improvised classroom, see? Small children, they draw here."

A wicker folding screen separates the school section from the rest of the house. There are three rocking chairs along the veranda and several potted plants on the floor against the wall. One basket with pale pink begonias hangs on the balcony rail. Outside the veranda is the yard with a giant mahogany in the center.

"Here is Cecilia," Fernando says.

"So glad you came!" She shakes my hand. Today her hair falls over her shoulders, giving her the look of a little girl.

"It's so pretty here," I say with sincerity.

"It's not so cold because the trees in this part of town protect us from the wind." She waves, showing the tree in the yard, accompanying each word with a gesture to make herself heard above the radio. I wonder why it occurs to no one to lower the volume.

Cecilia's eyes, like Fernando's, are large and soft. One feels embraced by their glance.

We stand against the rail. The terrain behind the house falls toward a valley, then climbs and becomes a bright green rolling hill with eucalyptus. In the distance the mountains are almost black in contrast.

Cecilia's face breaks into a warm smile every time our eyes meet. She seems as anxious for a friend as I am.

I feel excitement at the prospect of coming here every day. I see myself standing in front of the benches, the little hands of the children pulling at my skirt, touching my arm, asking questions.

Fernando's other sister comes out from one of the rooms along the veranda. "I am Elisa," she says, bowing formally, and does not shake my hand. I can see she's much older than Fernando and Cecilia. There are tiny wrinkles around her eyes, which don't glow like Cecilia's. Her braids are tightly wrapped around her head, the way she wears them to market.

"Mamacita is not feeling well today," she says, or rather shouts. "It's better not to tire her with too much talking."

I can't help wondering how sick the *mamacita* is if she can put up with the blaring radio. I notice that Elisa has been glancing at Fernando, trying to tell him something.

At last, moving closer to me, he says, "We don't need to tell Mama about your father, Marta, I mean his situation here and all that. If she asks questions, just say that your family is looking for land around here or that your family has moved here for a while."

Both Elisa and Cecilia are nodding their heads.

"But I don't want to lie, and I'm not ashamed of my father's actions. Perhaps I should come back some other time, when your mother is feeling better."

"Marta, Marta." Fernando smiles, reaching for my hand. "Don't be upset, no need—"

"Surely your mother has heard about my father in this place; her friends, everyone in this pueblo knows that he's the army's prisoner."

"Mama sees no one; she's an invalid," says Elisa.

81

"And your uncle? He must have told her about us."

"He's a busy person; he seldom comes to see us," Elisa and Fernando say simultaneously.

"Don't be upset, Marta." Cecilia's gentle and eager manner makes me smile. I look at Elisa, but she doesn't smile back. It's easy to guess that she has nothing to do with my coming to teach. It's she, however, who takes my arm and leads me toward her mother's room. Fernando and Cecilia are behind. The four of us advance along the veranda, our steps seemingly marching to the tempo of the radio's band, which grows louder. Cecilia is braiding her hair quickly, taking pins from her pocket, pinning them on the braid around her head. "Mamacita doesn't approve when I don't braid my hair," she says, looking at me.

I find myself standing at the door of a room cluttered with furniture: short-legged chairs; round and square small tables; crystal vases, one with red paper carnations. On a normal-sized chair a middle-aged woman sits, a blanket over her legs. She has the blackest eyes I have ever seen, or the dark circles beneath them give the impression that she's wearing a mask over her eyes.

"Come in, señorita, come in. My name is Paulina de Miranda," she says, extending her hand.

Muttering my name, I walk in quickly to receive her forceful grip; my ring presses painfully between my fingers.

"Find her a chair!"

Cecilia rushes to offer me a short-legged chair, which she places in front of her mother.

"Coffee, two cups!" Doña Paulina orders. Cecilia and Elisa dash to the door.

"You can manage alone, Elisa!"

Cecilia hesitates, then comes back to stand by my side.

"Come in, Fernando; don't stand by the door."

All is shouts and movement inside the room. I look up at Doña Paulina in her thronelike chair. She turns to the night table, which is between her chair and the large bed with a beige crocheted spread. At last she lowers the radio's volume slightly.

"There's a parade to commemorate the Battle of Boyacá," she explains.

She exudes the vitality of a young, healthy person. It occurs to me that it's her children who are the invalids.

"He's going to speak, you know," she says to me.

"Who?" I ask.

"The General."

The names of the streets through which the parade will pass on its way to the Presidential Plaza are being announced. Doña Paulina listens, her long fingers moving up and down. The band starts anew. Then her attention is all on me. The brilliant eyes survey me from head to foot.

"You are a teacher, Fernando tells me."

"Yes, Mama," he answers. He is still standing near the door. "Marta got her training at the Convent—"

"Did you get me the newspaper, son?"

"It's Saturday, Mama. The paper won't be here until noon."

"I got my training at the Normal Superior," Doña Paulina says, "years ago when teaching was a noble profession and the Normal's doors were open only to those who had a true vocation. I was principal of the Instituto Femenino de La Candelaria, the most distinguished college in the city, for years. That was all before your time, of course. On the wall behind you are some of my diplomas."

I turn. Several framed certificates and a silver medal against red velvet hang on the wall. I notice that Fernando is not in the room.

"I don't know about the salary," Doña Paulina continues

in her declamatory tone, punctuated by the drums of the band playing in the parade. "You see, señorita, the budget doesn't allow for an extra teacher, a helper, as my son suggests. You must understand that the appointment has to be approved by Colonel Ferreira and my brother; he is the mayor, you know, and the pay cannot be much." While speaking, she moves her fingers constantly, as though she were practicing a piano exercise. "You're familiar, no doubt, with teachers' salaries?"

I nod, feeling uncomfortable. I hadn't expected my visit to be a job interview.

Elisa walks in with a tray and two cups of coffee with milk and sugar already mixed in. She serves her mother, then me, and walks out, placing the tray at the foot of the bed.

We sip in silence.

"The American ambassador and other members of the diplomatic corps are taking their places on the presidential balcony, from which the General will soon address the nation," the announcer says in his stentorian voice.

"Hand me the Vicks VapoRub, Cecilia."

Cecilia, who has been standing by my side, goes to a corner of the room, to a table covered with all sizes of medicine jars and a thermos. I wonder why the table is placed so far from Doña Paulina's reach.

Cecilia begins rubbing her mother's neck with the Vicks, which gives off a pungent smell.

"Government of peace, progress, and prosperity," someone is yelling on the radio.

I am unaware of my grimace until Cecilia, now facing me, asks, "Something wrong, Marta?"

"The radio," I mutter softly, but she smiles as if I am complimenting the shiny, rectangular box and goes on massaging her mother.

"The salaries for teachers have never been generous. It's much better now under the General."

"My main interest, Doña Paulina, is to be busy and to help."

Doña Paulina puts out her moving-fingered hand to indicate that I have interrupted. "We have divided the children into three groups. I teach reading; Elisa and Cecilia, catechism and writing; and Fernando teaches arithmetic and some notions of history, the basics, of course. Rural education, you understand, so that they will not increase our country's illiteracy statistics and one day will be able to read the newspaper headlines and the names of the political candidates. Are you familiar with this type of teaching?"

"I heard my father once speak of this type of teaching!" I say with an anger I didn't realize I was feeling. "I'm not a teacher, really. I used to help the nuns read stories to the first- and second-graders, that's all."

"Very good! That's precisely what you would be needed for, to keep the little ones quiet while my son and my daughters and I teach."

Cecilia is finished with the rubbing and is giving a pill and a glass of water to Doña Paulina. Then, picking up the tray from the foot of the bed, she takes my empty cup and her mother's and walks out.

". . . democracy and glorious destiny of the nation." Someone is in the midst of a speech.

"I am an invalid, but I continue to teach. I have recommendations that could fill this room; that is the legacy I will leave to my children."

". . . historic action and progress."

Doña Paulina's voice and the one on the radio merge with each other, and for a moment I don't know whose words flood the room.

"If your appointment gets approved . . ." But she doesn't

finish, turning suddenly silent, her eyes fixed on my red ribbon. "Your hairdo—you notice my daughters'? A good appearance is very important in our profession."

I feel my face reddening.

She looks around. "Cecilia, where is everybody?" She raises her arms. I see many arms and hands with twisted fingers like tentacles; I have the vision of an octopus coming toward me.

"Thank you very much. I must go now." I stumble on the short-legged chair.

"Elisa, Cecilia!" she calls, and this time she turns off the radio. "Fernando!"

Quick steps approach on the veranda.

"Yes, Mama, sorry," Elisa and Cecilia say, the three entering the room.

"She has *no* teaching experience, Fernando. You told me she did."

His eyes dart toward me reproachfully.

"I'll see what I can do, señorita."

"Yes, I understand, thank you." I walk out.

Doña Paulina turns on the radio. Shouts of *"Viva el General"* and applause follow me to the veranda. I walk rapidly, Fernando and Elisa following.

I stop near the folding screen that separates their quarters from the school.

"If things can be arranged, will you consider coming, Marta?" Surprisingly, it is Elisa who asks.

"I'll see. I came today because I wanted to meet you." I look toward the tree in the center of the yard. "It's lovely here."

"Come back, Marta," Elisa says.

"Yes, adios."

"Wait, Marta, my hat. I'm coming with you," Fernando

says, but I walk through the classroom and out of the house.

Outside Fernando catches up with me. He holds my arm and we walk without speaking.

"You look distressed, Marta. What happened, did my mother say something?"

I shake my head.

"I'm sorry. It wasn't a good day. You see, her life, the radio is her only contact with the outside world."

"Of course, I understand."

"And you see, she said she would try her best."

"Yes, I know; I'm sure everything will be arranged." But Fernando doesn't capture the irony.

Ricardo is on the lane, coming toward us with Polo. It's not until I see my brother smiling at Fernando that I realize I haven't remembered about my father, to ask Fernando's help.

"Fernando!"

He stops at the urgency of my tone.

"Yes?"

"No, nothing."

"What is it, Marta?"

"Where does your mother buy her medicines?"

His face drops in disappointment at my question. "The army doctor, he gets all her prescriptions."

We stride toward the corner where Ricardo waits, looking at me with expectancy, still smiling.

囗 13

We rarely look at a calendar here, but this morning Papa takes out the small one he carries in his wallet. "Commemoration of the last battle against the Spaniards," he says. "I see; that's the reason for the racket next door."

The band at the base has been playing the national anthem.

"But the celebration was Saturday, Papa." I'm thinking of the parade on the radio while I visited Fernando's family.

"The official celebration was probably during the weekend, yes. The government is never short of pretexts to have parades, processions, unveiling of statues, anything to distract the public's attention from other happenings."

"They're marching around the flagpole," Ricardo says, coming from the backyard, "the clowns!"

"A year ago Eduardo Plata came to see me. Remember, Margarita? The night before, his older boy hadn't come home. For the next three days Eduardo and I visited every police department in the city, making inquiries. They knew no one by the name of Guillermo Plata, of course. They went through the mechanics of opening books, reading lists of the names of those who were apprehended or caught in the street after curfew." Papa pauses. "A week later Guillermo's body was discovered by two women on their way to mass. The boy had been tortured and beaten and was hardly recognizable."

"Miguel, must we speak—" Mama puts her hands on the edge of the bowl she has on her lap—she has been beating egg whites with a fork.

"I'm sorry, Margarita. Indeed, let's recall pleasurable things. José and Elvira were with us that afternoon, weren't they, and did we play croquet?"

"Miguel, really! Why mention José and my poor Elvira." She resumes beating with furious energy, *clickety-clickety-clickety-click.*

Mama shakes her head as she continues whipping. Guillermo Plata, José and Elvira, who else? she's probably thinking.

We all look at the bowl on her lap, the stiff, glossy whites she keeps punishing with the fork. Ricardo and Papa seem to be searching for something pleasant to say.

Names, dates, simple words have become dangerous among us. But I have a list of safe phrases:

The sky is gray.

Perico is growing.

My hair is long.

"Stop biting your nails, Ricardo!" Mama orders.

The villagers seem unaware of today's commemoration. The bell tolling and firecrackers are reserved for religious holidays.

The band has stopped, and now we hear a curse, followed by a crash. Someone is having an argument.

My father is suddenly absorbed in reading a typed page, but his eyes are fixed on the same spot. He is alert to the sounds coming from the base.

"We're lucky to have Pedrito. You think he'll come tonight, even if it's not Saturday?" Ricardo asks.

"Attend to your chicken, Ricardo. Get him out of here!" Mama is now moving around the kitchen.

"Pedro, yes, most probably. No reason to start getting apprehensive," Papa answers, looking apprehensive himself.

"What would you think, Papa, if Ricardo and I, or Ricardo alone, go to the city while the men at the base are having one of their fiestas, I mean on Saturday, for instance? He could sneak out and catch a bus on the main road and go to see Dr. Camacho. Then he could come back with the medicines the next Saturday when all the men at the base are drunk again. What would you think of something like that, Papa?"

He looks at me, steadily, then at Mama, frowning, as if he isn't sure of what he's just heard.

"You're not serious, Marta, I'm sure."

"I am serious."

"Listen, Marta, and listen well; you too, Ricardo." He folds the page he has been reading, slowly, and pushes it into his pocket, all the while looking from me to Ricardo. "As long as we don't do anything absurd, we'll probably be left alone, but one false move in that fantastic style you're proposing, Marta, will be enough for them to . . . to finish with the four of us. I'm sorry to say it so bluntly. Don't allow your imagination to—"

"You're right, Miguel," Mama says, stepping down to the yard, "but what about asking Pedro to deliver a letter to one of his friends, one of the truck drivers, for instance, who travels back and forth to the city, a letter to Camacho?"

"We'll do nothing of the sort! To give the soldier a letter is to expose him to death. I'm surprised you don't know any better, Margarita!"

We have locked ourselves in the living room as we always do on Saturday evenings. The laughter and singing of the men and their women friends at the base have been going on for hours.

We look forward to hearing Pedro's soft whistling, his way of letting us know that he's at the door watching, and to smelling his cheap cheroot, which filters through the window.

The radio is playing "Noche de Ronda" over and over. Ricardo says it must be a favorite of the colonel.

Ricardo and I doze on and off; Papa, as usual, walks about and coughs; and Mama moves her lips while she folds and unfolds the week's laundry.

At midnight we hear steps entering the house and a loud bang on the living room door.

"Open the door!" We recognize Pedro's voice, but his insolent tone gives us a start. *"¡Abra la puerta!"*

We all go to the door, and Papa removes the latch.

The stench of alcohol takes us aback. Pedro doesn't greet us and keeps looking fixedly at Papa. A bottle of rum bulges in his pants pocket.

Pretending that nothing is unusual, my father thanks him for watching over us, asking if he would like a cup of coffee.

Pedro doesn't answer but continues to stare, his nostrils flaring.

"Good night, Pedrito," my father finally says.

Pedro puts out his hand to push the door that Papa is slowly closing. "My godfather Don Honorio is dead!" The echo resounds in the room, dead . . . dead.

"Honorio?" My father reacts at last. "You say Honorio is dead? How? When? Explain yourself, Pedro."

"It's her fault!" Pedro points at me. "She talked to my *padrino* at the market. Everybody saw her, Polo told me. That's why my godfather got killed!"

I cover my face and begin crying.

"Honorio came bringing some herbs for you, Papa," Ricardo explains.

"When? Did you know about this, Margarita?"

"No, Miguel, I didn't know."

"Honorio? He talked to you, Marta, my old friend Honorio, and you said nothing to me or to your mother?" He pushes my hand down, away from my face. "Speak up, Marta!" Odd that I am thinking, How can the voice of a sick man be so strong?

"I am waiting!"

It's Ricardo who speaks: "He just gave Marta a bunch of herbs, you know, dry herbs, like he used to—"

"I was—Ricardo and I—I was going to tell you, Papa, but I saw Honorio leaving the plaza with two officers. I didn't want to worry you."

I wait for someone to speak.

"You couldn't have done anything, Miguel," Mama says finally, her arm around my shoulders.

"You should have told me instead of keeping it a secret. I wonder what other secrets you're both—"

"None, Papa!" Ricardo and I say at the same time.

"The day my *padrino* was going back to Arroyo they got him at the market and took him in a jeep to the barracks up there on the mountain. The people from around there saw what happened. Two campesinos trying to defend my godfather; they were also shot. Last week I was sent there on duty. Teniente Rojas asked us to do the 'cleaning,' that's what they call it, the *limpieza* on the road. We found his body already stinking; the buzzards were beginning to get busy with it." Pedro leans his rifle against the doorway and fumbles inside his pocket. "Here," he says, unwrapping a soiled, smelly handkerchief. "I have his gold tooth." The tooth gleams in the semidarkness of the room. Attached to it, hanging like a tassel, is a piece of bloodless gum.

Mama gasps, turning her head. Ricardo and I cannot take our eyes away.

"Put it aside, Pedro," Papa orders.

"It's the campesinos who get murdered and raped. It's not the señores like you. See?" he shouts. "You're alive and well." He's waving his arm toward Mama and me.

Papa motions for us to go back to our chairs. He talks softly, explaining to Pedro that we're all under a regime of terror. "It's not only the campesinos. Many of my friends have been tortured and killed in the city." Has Honorio's family been informed, is there a way he can help? he goes on asking.

"They know it, yes."

"Are guerrillas fighting up there where Honorio was killed?"

"There's no fighting, nothing. Every week is the same. Colonel Ferreira or Captain Paredes and the officers, they hunt and get drunk and rape the campesinas, a boy also the other day. Teniente Gómez, he likes boys."

"Honorio was here because of me. It's my fault, of course. His family!" Papa mutters softly, talking to himself.

"Yes, Señor Don Miguel, it's your fault. He was like my father." Pedro is wiping his nose with the back of his hand. "It's the campesinos," he repeats.

"My health, you see?" My father's voice is barely audible. "It's a matter of time, Pedro; they don't need to kill me." He stretches his arms to embrace Pedro. "My sympathy."

Half stumbling, the soldier moves backward to avoid Papa's embrace. Then, picking up his rifle, he starts to leave.

Ricardo darts to the door. "It's not my father's fault, Pedrito. He didn't ask your *padrino* to come."

Papa pats Ricardo's shoulder, turning away from the door toward his chair, near Mama's. "I don't know."

"Surely you're not blaming yourself, Miguel. It's not your fault that they're murderers," Mama says.

"But why must he tell us that soon it'll be all over?" I

address my question to Mama as if my father isn't there with us.

Shaking his head, he keeps mumbling the same words, *"I don't know."*

"Honorio, he was your friend, but the others, Hernández and Posada and Villegas and all those who came to our house to see you, they don't care. What have they done for us? They needed you when you were important." I go on calling them cowards, hypocrites, and every word that comes into my mind, pausing from time to time to see my father's reaction. Resentment against him overcomes me. I'm aware that throughout my outburst I want to force Papa to tell me one of his optimistic phrases: "We mustn't despair. We'll be home soon; you'll see."

"Why don't you answer, Papa?"

"How do you think your father is feeling, Marta? Honorio has been a dear old friend since before you were born. You've said enough; keep quiet now."

"Say something, Papa, please."

He presses his fist to his forehead and closes his eyes. Two tears roll down his face. "This helplessness," he whispers hoarsely. Mama moves her chair closer to his.

For a while my sniffling is the only sound in the room. The music coming from the base sounds louder.

"Noche de ronda . . ."

"There it goes again." Papa smiles, looking from Mama to me, trying to ease our mood. "The colonel's musical number."

I doze on and off, finally falling asleep in my chair. Then I am awakened by my mother's shout, "Ricardo, where is Ricardo?" She and my father are standing near the door.

"He's somewhere near, Margarita."

"What happened?" I ask.

"We can't find him!" Papa and my mother answer at the same time. I follow them, also calling, shouting into the dark hill, "Ricardo!"

We come back into the house and rush toward the backyard. The bulbs around the base yard illuminate the embankment that separates our house from the military quarters. Ricardo is nowhere. An officer and a prostitute are leaning against the flagpole, embracing and laughing. Inside the base someone smashes a bottle.

"Margarita, Marta, let's go in." Papa takes us by the arm, and we return to the house.

"You think he's all right, Papa?"

"I'm sure he's all right," Papa says. The thought that Ricardo may be in his room comes to the three of us, and we run along the corridor.

Mama pushes the door and turns on the ceiling bulb, but the cot, the only furniture in the room, is empty. On top of it are the wooden sticks used for Perico's jumping act and a notebook with a drawing of the plaza on market day that Ricardo has been sketching all week: a multitude of tiny peasants' hats, like dots floating over the plaza, the church tower, and the mountains in the background.

As we leave his room, we see the chicken in the front yard, perched on the old board shelter my brother built.

"Ricardo! Ricardo!" Mama keeps calling.

"Listen, Margarita." My father grabs her by the shoulder. "Stop it, please. Ricardo is convincing Pedro that it's not my fault about Honorio. You see, the boy can't face losing our only friend in this place. He must be nearby."

Back in the living room, Mama rushes to the window one moment; the next, she paces back and forth, her lips moving in prayer.

My father leaves the room, murmuring something. After a

moment he comes back wearing his hat and with a pair of shoes in his hands.

"Look, Miguel, soon it'll be daylight and Ricardo . . . What are we going to do?"

Papa doesn't answer for a moment while he takes off his slippers and steps into his shoes. "You two wait here. I have an idea. I'll be back shortly."

"No, please. What's the matter with you, Miguel? Someone will see you!"

"There's no one around, Margarita. See, the music has stopped. They're all sleeping. No one will see me!"

Mama and I go to the window. My father is a dark shadow moving downhill, disappearing under the crest.

A cock crows nearby. Simultaneously, two cocks answer in the distance, and the air begins to fill with the crowing of roosters. The lights around the plaza have been turned off.

We move back and forth from our chairs to the window.

"Let's be quiet for a moment, Mama. Everything will be all right."

But she doesn't hear me and keeps moving about and pausing by the window.

The sound of Perico's flapping and clucking comes into the room.

"Marta, I think . . . Yes, they're coming. Thank God!" My father's hunched figure is emerging from downhill. Close to him is Ricardo and behind him, Pedro, the three figures ascending against the mother-of-pearl sky.

"But what's the matter with Ricardo?" asks Mama.

Ricardo is staggering, as if his legs are giving out. Holding his arm, Papa is having a difficult time of it.

Mama covers her face and begins uttering gurgling sounds.

Why is she crying now? I wonder. Then I see that she's

chuckling softly. "He's drunk; Ricardo is drunk! Look, Mama, he's stumbling all over like Pedro!"

She nods but can't speak through her chuckles, which grow louder into bursts of laughter, our laughter that keeps pouring, rich and generous, like a cascade restoring new life to arid soil.

As they come closer, I notice my brother's ashen face and the stupor in his wide-open eyes.

"Come, let's help Papa." But we don't leave the window, shaking, clutching at each other. We can't stop laughing.

14

The *clack-clack* of my father's old Remington has become like music in this place. When he pauses for a long time, our eyes dart from one to another, and we interrupt what we are doing until the typewriter's clatter resumes.

But in the last weeks, since we heard the news about Honorio, my father spends much time in the hammock, an empty stare in his eyes.

We've been going to the market at dawn, to avoid Fernando and his sisters or anyone who risks being our friend, like Honorio.

The soldier grumbles every Saturday, "The burros are not even unloaded, and the good fruits come in the trucks later."

Gazing ahead, Ricardo and I move on, answering greetings from the campesinos, smiling, yet looking no one in the eye. The campesinos have turned friendly since the day the mayor's nephew strolled around the plaza by my side.

"You come so early, señorita."

I smile and nod and don't look at the campesina from whom I am buying vegetables.

"The cold don't go to your bones?"

I feign concentration as I throw carrots and yuccas in the basket.

"Where is your chicken, niño?" an old campesina calls to

Ricardo. "You don't bring him to the market no more? Did you eat him?"

Ricardo shakes his head quickly.

"Here, thank you, good-bye," I say, and we move on.

"Señorita, come!" A pretty young campesina calls me. "I sell you this shawl my aunt made." She wraps around her head a plain, bright pink shawl with a black fringe. "You like it?" She grins, showing her gums with two teeth. Dropping her voice, she tells me that the Señor Profesor asked about me last Saturday. "I told him you come early now, when the hens are still snoring."

I pretend I'm not interested and go on picking up oranges and bananas.

"Try it, señorita, the shawl."

I put it on my head briefly, holding it under my chin.

"How pretty you look!" the campesina and the other women nearby chorus.

I don't have enough money today to buy such a lovely shawl, I say, and, paying for the oranges and bananas, I walk away, followed by Ricardo and Polo.

At this hour there are no military men or villagers at the plaza, and the peasants visit with one another. The women giggle, gossip, and are forever telling each other of the last week's deceased. "She died so *contenta*," they say, sighing, repeating the phrase over and over, as if they are envious of the departed one's contentment. The men, in separate groups, play harmonicas and pull from their *mochilas*—colorful hemp bags they all carry—bottles for their first *aguardiente* (firewater) of the day.

They have become familiar, these peasants: the woman who sells the pottery, with a goiter the size of a soccer ball; the stout one with the three small children, one clutching her neck, another her arm, and the littlest sucking her breast, like three monkeys clinging to a tree; the many

Marias, who are each identified by a nickname—Maria the String Bean, Big-eyed Maria, and Maria the Sad One, who never smiles; and the young campesinas, whose way of flirting is by braiding and unbraiding their hair.

There is an old, toothless peasant, who laughs in a quiet, high-pitched "hee-hee-hee," wiping his tiny red eyes with a flowered bandana. "Ñor Crisanto," the others call him, as if it's not proper to use the whole word *señor* to address a campesino. "Dark skies, Ñor Crisanto." Maybe the old peasant is not laughing, I say to myself; maybe he's crying with his strange, high-pitched "hee-hee-hee."

Now that I talk only to my family, I am eager to visit with everyone around. I don't mind their garlic breath and decaying teeth anymore. Sometimes I have to push my hands inside my cardigan pockets to remind myself not to touch them.

The little store where we buy Papa's aspirins doesn't open until seven. I tell Mama every week that we should buy a larger stock of aspirins, but she insists I get only the week's supply every Saturday, as if it's fresh eggs we are buying. "Maybe we'll hear something, and we'll be able to go home or place Miguel in a hospital. Who knows?" We must be careful with our expenses, she also says, and I've noticed how the shopping list grows smaller each week.

"Look who's coming, Marta." Ricardo nudges me. I see Fernando striding toward us. I hesitate between my desire to speak to him and an inner voice warning, "Go home; be sensible."

"I'll go ahead, Ricardo. Here's the money for the aspirins; you wait until the store opens."

"You're not going anyplace by yourself, Señorita Marta," Polo retorts. Since we've been coming to the plaza early, he is bad-tempered, yelling at us, sometimes not helping me, as he did before, to carry the basket.

Fernando is now in front of me. "Why are you avoiding me, Marta?" he asks immediately. "I've looked for you here at the market the past weeks. I've been worried about you. Elisa and Cecilia also. Even Mama asked about you the other day. Let me help you," he says, bending to take the basket I am carrying, and then, turning to the soldier, he calls, "You here, help the señorita."

"*Sí, Señor Profesor.*" Polo rushes to take the basket from him.

"You mustn't be seen talking to us, Fernando. You can get yourself into trouble, and your family."

He scowls as if he doesn't understand what I'm talking about. "I miss you, Marta."

I walk to the little store, which is now being opened. He follows me. The zipper of my change purse is caught, and my hand shakes as I force it.

"Let me do it." He grabs my hand and looks at me.

"Please, give it to me," I say, jerking my hand away. He tries to move the zipper one way and then the other, finally untangling it.

The store owner has already placed the usual number of aspirin envelopes on the counter.

"How are you this cold morning, señorita?" His little eyes shine, and he is smiling, looking from Fernando to me. "Señor Profesor, good morning." Do I want anything else? he asks, looking toward the barrels of rice, beans, and other grains lined up against the wall, near the door.

"A school notebook, please."

There's enough paper at the house, but Ricardo and I are always buying the notebooks, as if paper, like the aspirins and the alcohol, is also medicine for Papa.

Polo takes the paper bag containing the aspirins and the school notebook from the counter and puts it in the basket. He doesn't have the sullen expression of a moment ago—

Fernando's presence breaks the monotony of these past weeks at the market.

"Marta, we've bought everything; we can go now," Ricardo says. He is already outside the store.

"Come, Marta, let's take a walk. I have something to tell you," Fernando invites me, taking my arm.

I hesitate, but to stroll around the plaza with Fernando is suddenly a temptation I can't resist. "You're taking a risk; you know it." Quickly I tell him about Honorio. ". . . just because they saw him talking to me, giving me some dry herbs, they killed him!"

Fernando's expression doesn't change. He doesn't say "How cruel" or "Poor man." He doesn't say "It'll soon be over. The newspapers report rebellions against the government breaking out everywhere." Fernando says nothing.

After a moment, he says, "Nothing will happen to me or to my family, and in any case, I'm not afraid."

"And why should you be afraid, indeed? Your uncle—"

"I wish you would detach me from my uncle, Marta. We're two different people."

"Wait for me, Ricardo. I'm coming!" I turn to my brother, who is still standing in the same place, waiting. Polo hasn't moved away from my side.

"I have something to tell you, Marta. Come." Fernando takes my arm, and once more I move along with him.

"I wrote to the colonel asking for permission for you to be our assistant teacher. I got my mother to sign it as the school principal. In the letter I explained that you've had teaching experience."

"You shouldn't have done it. They'll ask for recommendations, and I have none. But mainly because of my father, you shouldn't have done it."

"You don't need any recommendations. My uncle will

take care of everything. I'm going to speak to him. The letter is just a formality."

Why do I go along with this? I ask myself. His uncle, his mother, they are all supporters of the man who is killing my father slowly. Does loneliness justify my behavior? "No, no," I hear myself saying aloud, answering myself.

"Yes, Marta! I want to see you. I miss you!"

"It's because there's no one else for you or me here; that's why we— you think you miss me."

"Look, Marta, two hours away in Marañón there are many pretty girls. I used to go often. It's only a matter of catching a bus, but I'd rather be here near you."

I am suddenly aware of an unusual silence around us. The harmonicas and the chanting of the peasants nearby have stopped. Everyone is still, their eyes on Fernando and me.

He frowns at our wide-eyed audience. "Can you try to slip out of the house some afternoon this week and come to the plaza? During the week there's no one around, and we can talk."

"What a question. Really! Of course I can't get out, Fernando. How little you seem to know. Even talking to you in front of all these people is wrong, risky. I have to think of my father."

"Your father, your father," he whispers harshly.

Behind us Ricardo and Polo are arguing. My brother is telling the soldier that he's a poor excuse for an escort. "You're not supposed to allow my sister to talk to anyone. I'm going home!" he says loudly enough for me to hear, and this time he walks away.

Polo remains at my heels. Like the villagers and the campesinos, his curiosity about the mayor's nephew and me dominates him. Fernando and I are the circus coming to town.

But suddenly Fernando seems uneasy. He draws back, then stops to pull a cigarette out of his pocket. "You're right, Marta. It's better not to see each other here. We should wait until we get an answer from Colonel Ferreira." He keeps fanning the match, as he looks away from me. I follow his gaze. The mayor, at the corner and surrounded as usual by a group of locals, is staring in our direction.

"Think of what I say, Marta. Maybe you can escape for an hour or so during the week. Please try! Adios."

A peasant girl giggles.

"Shhhh." Several women rebuke the girl.

Fernando presses my hand quickly with his left hand while holding the cigarette with the other, flicking the ashes. He walks away hastily, leaving me standing there by myself.

There is a deep "Ahhhh," a sigh of disappointment coming from the women around.

"¡Vamos!" Polo yells, frustrated as well at the flat ending between the mayor's nephew and the señorita. "Pronto, I have things to do!" His eyes dart toward the corner, at the mayor.

Ricardo is standing on the other side of the plaza by the corner of the little street that leads to the main road.

My brother and I don't speak to each other as we climb the hill. We stop near the house, at the spot where we normally hear the typewriter. But today no sound comes through the window. We approach the house quickly, both filled with the same apprehension.

Polo places the basket on the ground and leaves. Papa coughs, and we know he is in the hammock. We hesitate by the door—every Saturday when we come back from the market Papa seems diminished, as though he melts while we are away.

The trick is not to catch him off guard, not to see his eyes staring into space, his sunken cheeks trembling as he mutters to himself.

"Here we are!" we announce, marching into the house, each carrying a basket.

We look at the hammock slowly. First to his hat, the gray, crumpled hat pulled down over his eyebrows. Then quickly to his feet, the points of his slippers showing under the blanket that covers his legs, to the poncho and the plaid woolen scarf, and finally to his chin. The face has grown so small that one can see it all with eyes fixed on the chin. The trick is not to have an overall view of our shrunken father in the hammock.

"Here you are. How was the plaza today?"

"Fine." We tell him someone asked about Perico, as if we are reporting a great occurrence.

"There he is, my *compañero*!" He signals to one corner of the yard, where the chicken is pecking.

Mama comes from the backyard, her arms filled with dry laundry. "Did you get everything?" she asks, looking from me to Ricardo and back to me with expectancy. She means, Did you see anybody who could help with your father's medicines?

Ricardo begins an imitation of the campesinos chanting their products in diminutive, *"Los huevitos frescos, las naranjitas dulces, los tomaticos rojos."* Mama and I laugh, but the audience in whose honor he is performing is not listening. He moves closer to the hammock, repeating, "Fresh little eggs, sweet little oranges, little red tomatoes." My father pushes away the blanket and gets out of the hammock.

"Where are you going, Miguel?"

He looks at Mama, somewhat startled by the alarm in her tone.

"I'm going to . . . to the typewriter," he says.

Mama sighs with relief and, pressing the bundle of clothes to her bosom, she walks ahead of him into the living room.

Ricardo and I go to the kitchen to empty the baskets. The three of us move with animation at the prospect of listening to the music of the old Remington.

⌷ 15

My mother and I sit by the window. Papa's cough is muffled by the closed doors of his bedroom and the living room.

Now and then Mama looks up from the shirt she's mending and follows my eyes, gazing down at the dark, solitary figure strolling around and around the plaza, disappearing momentarily under the crest of the hill, emerging again by the side of the church. It's Fernando.

He has been coming every day for the past week—my dear sentinel. I can't distinguish his features from here, yet it's as if I were looking at his face through binoculars, so clearly do I see it: the scar like a miniature half-moon beneath his right eye, his full lips. I want to stretch my hand, as though I could reach the plaza and touch his face.

"It's your Señor Profesor, isn't it?" my mother asks, a hint of irony in her tone. "Ricardo has told me that he looks for you at the market." Then, lowering her voice, as if inviting me to confide, she inquires if I still see him now that we go to the market so early.

"Last Saturday we spoke briefly. He— well, we just saw each other for a moment."

She moves her lips and I wait for her comment, but she says nothing.

I wish to tell her that Fernando wrote a letter to Colonel Ferreira asking authorization for me to become an assistant to him and his sisters in the local school, tell her how I would like to get out of this house for a few hours every day, and what does she think of the idea? Would she help me to convince my father? I want to confide to my mother my desire and my reluctance to have something develop between Fernando and me. Often, by this window, I find myself thinking that I need a girlfriend more than a mother, someone with whom I can laugh and who would listen to my secrets.

My mother is like a defenseless creature in the woods that, at a certain hour of the day, ventures out but whom the slightest noise frightens back into her lair.

"Mama, tell me about you and Papa when you were young and first met each other."

"Come now, Marta. You've heard—"

"Tell me again."

She smiles, pleased to repeat a story she has often told me. Mama always says it with the same words, changing nothing. "Your father had just graduated from law school. My brother Alberto was his classmate. One afternoon he brought your father to our house. Unlike other friends of Alberto's, who flirted with me behind his back, Miguel said, 'I would like to meet your sister.' My family didn't quite approve of the short, dark man with the flower in his lapel who was always talking about his peasant ancestry. 'There he is again, Margarita's campesino,' they would say, and 'Why doesn't he associate himself with a law firm like Alberto instead of writing those controversial articles for the local paper? That's the trouble,' they would comment. 'A peasant is lucky enough to get accepted to the university and then, once there, he becomes intoxicated by strange ideas.'

"When we were spending the holidays in our house by the sea, Miguel asked permission to visit me. Saturday evenings he would appear at the house. My parents and whoever was at the house spending the weekend would sit in the living room with Miguel and me. One night he spoke about his family, of an army regiment encamping on their farm at the time of a civil revolt. His father refused to join and to fight for a cause he didn't understand. The army took the horses and the cattle, then set fire to the house. Miguel was a child then. His mother saved him and herself by hiding in a hole in the ground where the tobacco leaves were stored. They never saw his father again.

"Priests were venerated in those days. Miguel's mother sent him to the seminary. How else was her campesino son going to make it? Miguel didn't have a vocation and convinced his mother to allow him to transfer to the National University. To become a lawyer was not what he wanted either. 'My ambition,' he'd say, 'is to combat the tactics and machinations of our country's rulers.' But you see, Marta, there was no such thing as a school of journalism then.

"My family would make no comment at the end of Miguel's stories. That silence! To my ears it sounded like the ocean outside crashing against the walls. Miguel did not seem perturbed by it. 'I'll see you next Saturday, Margarita.' Those were the only words he was able to say to me, really.

" 'Saturday we'll hear the next installment of the life of Margarita's campesino,' my family would tease. But slowly they began accepting Miguel. Why, they looked forward to his visits." Mama smiles and shakes her head as she always does at the conclusion of her narration.

I think of Papa's brief version of their courtship. He compared my mother to a pearl locked between stubborn shells. ". . . and then one day the shells gave in, the pearl leaped out, and I, the sea worm, skimmed away with my treasure."

Now I look at my mother. Reminiscence is still in her eyes. After a moment she resumes her darning. Her hand oscillates as the needle goes on weaving on the cloth. The wedding rings are loose on her finger, which has grown thin, bony, and slightly twisted by arthritis. I notice for the first time a freckle like a fly on her pale hand. I have an impulse to take my mother's hand and kiss it. I want to ask, one day, Mama, will I also sit with my own daughter, answering her questions, telling her my memories? Mostly I need my mother's reassurance that this prison and the fate of my sick father won't scar my life forever.

Fernando is now standing in front of the cantina. He's holding on to his hat with both hands to save it from a gust of wind.

"How awful for that young man to live in this pueblo," Mama says. "I mean, for us, dreadful as it is, we know that we're here for a limited period until the dictator . . . but he and his sisters. Ricardo told me he has two sisters?"

"And their mother is an invalid."

"How terrible!" Mama stops mending and looks at Fernando, still in front of the cantina, his head toward us.

"My pity is for him and his sisters," I say. "Their mother, well, she's lived her life. I'm sure she has plenty to remember, but they—"

"They're young, Marta. Life is ahead of them." She pats my knee.

"What if the dictator is never overthrown? I would grow old here, you know, Ricardo and I. You and Papa—I mean, you've lived your lives."

"Like the invalid mother of your friend? Is that what you mean, Marta? But life is not a meal that gluts you and of which you say, 'Enough!' Your father and I—we also have

110

dreams, projects. . . . At our ages every day, every hour, becomes more precious. These months here . . . his . . ." Her voice becomes soft, the last words unintelligible. She looks down at the brick floor. "Miguel," she muses.

Fernando is moving around the plaza.

"I wanted to go on speaking to him last Saturday," I'm saying, more to myself. "Such a simple thing, to talk to the only friend I have in this pueblo."

"You must be careful, Marta. Don't encourage his feelings. You mustn't forget our position here."

"I know, I know."

We don't speak for a while. Then she says, "Why don't you let Ricardo and the soldier do the shopping by themselves? You could stay in bed and sleep late. Wouldn't you like that?"

"But going to the market—that's my only outing!"

"No need to shout; it was only a suggestion." Mama looks at her darning, cuts the thread with her teeth, and sticks the needle in her blouse. "I don't need to tell you, Marta, that whatever attraction you imagine you feel for this young man, it's simply because he's the only one in the pueblo. Even the impossibility of visiting with him at the market, such a simple thing, as you said, increases your attraction. Under normal circumstances, in the city, for instance, would your choice be this Fernando?"

I look away. Fernando is not in the plaza anymore. My eyes on the crest of the hill, I wait, hoping to see him emerge. But the plaza is empty.

"We'll pretend that you are both journalists working for me," Papa said to Ricardo and me this week. "Your first assignment will be to outline your projects for when we leave this place."

I realize that lately Ricardo and I make plans for the future only when Papa is around; that is, we play scenes in the little yard. In the beginning we were always telling each other the things we were going to do after we were back home, free. Forgiving our friends was one of them. "They rejected us because they were afraid, that's all, no punishment. 'Clemency granted,'" Ricardo would say. He couldn't wait to be back home playing soccer with Lucho and Guillermo and the other boys on the block. "And to go to the stadium with Papa on Sunday!"

"Just to walk the streets, Ricardo, to go to our own parish Sunday morning and then to the park to listen to the band concert. And we used to think that was boring, remember?"

Then one day, in unison, my brother and I stopped making plans for the future, and to recall the past brought tears to our eyes. Thus we ended by saying nothing. We understood that conversation has no significance without memories and projects. Like the hammock in the yard that is supported with ropes at both ends, conversation, life itself, is suspended between evocations and dreams.

But we still talk about our future in front of Papa. Then it's a matter of following our instinct or Mama's eyes. She enlarges them with approval when we speak as if at any moment one of our friends or Uncle Alberto will burst into the house, calling, "Get ready. Come, let's go. It's all over!"

"I'm not going to bother packing my clothes," I said the other day. "They're so worn out. I'll just jump into the car with whatever clothes I have on . . . when they come!"

"Right, Marta. I'll take back only my madeira tablecloth and napkins. Why did I ever pack such things, really!" Mama forgot that to mention them was to bring to mind Papa's poorly organized plot to leave the country. She packed her fine tablecloth to entertain the wives of my father's friends in Costa Rica.

She's a bad actress, Mama. Ricardo and I cringe at her

performances in the little yard. She talks to Papa as though he's a child to whom she's promising a picnic. "Miguel, one thing we'll do when we go home is to spend a week or so by the sea. You always feel so well there."

"Yes, Margarita, yes," he used to say at first, winking at us and patting her hand. He doesn't do any of that anymore. He keeps looking at a fixed point in front of him.

I notice that Ricardo, like me, follows his gaze, as if to discover what Papa's eyes see: the streets of our cities without soldiers? His friends free and alive? His paper circulating openly? Does he see the valleys and mountains of our country bursting with clean, prosperous, and smiling campesinos working their own parcels of land? Are Mama, Ricardo, and I somewhere in the paradise of his vision? But I reproach myself for assuming that the visions of my father have only a political dimension.

He speaks of a dream he had the other night. Mama was bringing a tray from the kitchen, "as when you offer us one of your delicious dishes, Margarita."

"Ground beef with rice? Or ground beef with yucca?" Ricardo asks, referring to what Mama gives us more and more lately.

"You're interrupting, Ricardo. As I was saying, you had this tray, Margarita, but when you lowered it, I saw that it wasn't food you were offering us, but books, a tray full of books! Novels, biographies, adventures, books of every size!"

"Books?" Mama and I say at the same time, glancing at each other, finding nothing remarkable about his dream.

"The dream, of course, is because I keep wondering how to get ahold of reading material. What a difference it would make to have something to read. I've been thinking that perhaps through Pedro we could mail an order to the Villa Real bookstore in the city. . . ."

Mama, who has been chopping onions with that obsessive energy she puts into every action, drops the knife on the table and strides to the center of the yard to stand in front of the hammock.

"Miguel, you forbid me to use the soldier to send a letter to Dr. Camacho, asking for medicines, and now you speak about sending an order for books with Pedro? Books, Miguel, really! Are they more important than your health?"

"They are, Margarita. They'll be a medication for all of us, to keep our minds"—he points toward Ricardo and me—"away from our surroundings. We all need that. But of course we shouldn't expose Pedro to any risk. It was just an idea."

Before finishing what he's saying, he is overcome by a fit of coughing. It's a barking cough, shaking him, the hammock, shaking the whole yard, it seems. We all watch him, even Perico—one leg lifted, the chicken stands immobile, his head inclined toward my father.

Ricardo is anxious to read his composition; he keeps looking at his pages. He won't start until Mama stops what she's doing in the kitchen and comes to sit in her chair.

"Go ahead; I'm all ears," Mama says.

In his constant effort to make us laugh, Ricardo describes the political caricatures that appeared in the newspapers before the General was elected. The subject of most of them was "the beautifying of our Presidential candidate," with his new teeth; his stylized pompadour; and his bright, gold-rimmed glasses. But the caricature Ricardo describes in detail is the one in which the General, in the body of a fat woman, clutches a bedpost while two men pull up on his corset. Many identified my father as one of the men pulling the corset strings. Ricardo's composition ends, "What the General needed was a new heart."

He looks up from the paper to Papa first, then to Mama,

a tentative smile on his face; he is expecting some word of approval.

Nobody speaks.

Ricardo looks at me inquiringly.

"Five years ago," Papa says at last, "that caricature came out at the time his campaign was gaining force. I was convinced then that he was the right man. You remember well, Ricardo. You were only what . . . seven, eight?"

"Let's hear your composition, Marta," Mama says quickly.

I mumble about not having it ready. "I couldn't finish it. . . . Next Sunday."

"I saw you writing. You must have something in that notebook of yours. You're always scribbling. Go on," she insists.

I'm looking at Papa, who has been rereading Ricardo's paper.

The heavy atmosphere of every Sunday afternoon descends upon the yard.

"We almost forgot. Today is haircut day!" Mama says with childish animation. She goes to get the scissors and comes back.

Papa puts his hand out. He and Ricardo can wait another week for her barbershop services. He would like to go to his room and take a rest before dinner. "Call me when it's time to eat, Margarita."

Mother motions with her eyes, and Ricardo immediately helps Papa to his feet. Holding his arm, he guides Papa to the door of the bedroom.

"It's good, what you wrote, Ricardo, well observed," he says softly.

Mama's hand smooths her skirt and keeps smoothing it over and over as if she cannot stop. As she sees Ricardo coming back to the yard, she says, "Of all things to write about, Ricardo, why did you choose that?"

"What did I do wrong now?"

"Don't shout! I can think of so many other subjects. Why always this . . . politics? Don't you have things you want to do in the future? Don't you want to be home or back in school with friends . . . to replace your wasted time here? Are you planning to be a chicken trainer for the rest of your life?"

Ricardo is biting his lips to stop them from trembling.

"When I was your age and Marta's, I had many interests. I was able to speak of different things."

"What did you speak about, Mama?" I ask.

"Trips, clothes, games, social life. Frivolous conversation, I suppose, but my brother Alberto and I and our friends, we weren't obsessed with politics. Of all things to write about!"

"He didn't know the meaning of that stupid cartoon, Mama," I say. "He was eight years old at that time, eight years."

"You children don't understand; you simply don't understand!" And she stretches her lips into the tight-mouthed smile that makes my brother and me look away.

"What's for dinner, Mama?"

"Heavens, Marta, you've asked that question a dozen times. Dinner is chicken with rice. It will be our last taste of chicken!" Then she adds, "There's hardly money left for our expenses."

16

To postpone their congratulations and well-wishing, I lie on my cot, watching the never-ending procession of ants between the brick floor and the roof.

"We want to see you, Marta. It's late!" Mama calls.

"Come in!"

"Happy birthday!" Mama and Ricardo kiss me, she thrusting into my hand a small tissue package—the paper alone is a rarity here. She probably had it in her suitcase, wrapping lingerie or a piece of jewelry.

I unfold it carefully. My mother is giving me her earrings, two sapphires inside gold filigreed circles.

"I always meant to give them to you. Your eighteenth birthday is a good occasion." She asks me to put them on, and we both fidget as we take off my pearls. I don't know if I am more touched by my mother's generosity or by the roughness of her fingertips, which were once cotton-soft.

"They look lovely on you." She turns my face this way and that.

Ricardo looks on, sliding back one foot first, then the other, as if he is a bull about to launch against the matador—his manner when he wants to hide his emotions.

Mama pushes me toward the mirror, which is now hanging on the wall of my room since Ricardo and I hardly go into Papa's bedroom.

"Come, your father's in the living room." Mama explains that last night when it began raining, she woke up Ricardo and they hooked the hammock there. "We won't be able to sit outside anymore."

Our little yard is sodden with mud, fit only for Perico's spidery feet. I look at it with nostalgia, recalling our first months here: Sunday's English lessons and Papa's efforts to make us laugh, his optimistic conversations with Ricardo, our chairs around my father, as if the hammock were a fireplace to warm us. Will the past, even the past in this ugly house, will it always be better than the present? I wonder, heaving a deep sigh like Mama's.

"Will we use the yard again some day, Mama?"

"Don't be silly, Marta. Of course. But who knows, maybe by the time the dry season returns, we'll be gone!"

"Today is your birthday, Marta!" my father says as we walk into the room.

I bend to receive his kiss, but he pats my head.

It occurs to me that his salutation without the word *happy* is appropriate—today is your birthday.

"Sit here, Marta." Mama shows me a chair.

I would be more comfortable near the window, Papa says, and for a moment they fuss over me as if I were a visitor.

Ricardo leaves, announcing he's going to get his gift.

My sixteenth birthday comes to my mind. We spent it in the green house by the sea that we rented every year when Doctor Camacho advised rest for my father. It was the fishing season, the fiesta of San Pedro.

From the porch we would see silver mackerels darting under radiant skies. At night the fishermen played drums, flutes, and maracas on the beach. They danced the *cumbia* in a circle, each holding a candle, trying to keep it glowing against the wind.

My mother and I took turns dancing with Papa on our porch.

One early morning from the balcony I saw my parents on the beach. My mother in her light, colorful dress; close to her, Papa with dark clothes and scarf and hat, his usual attire, which made other bathers turn and stare. But that morning there was no one else on the beach, only the two of them, and gulls flying close to the shore. My mother moved with buoyancy. In the distance she was like a kite. Holding hands, they separated from time to time to bend and pick up stones and little crabs, Mama throwing her head backward as she laughed. Then I saw a change, as when a blue, sunny sky turns stormy abruptly. Mama returned toward our house; my father tried to catch up with her. As they came near, the wind brought his voice to my ears. "Wait, Margarita, wait!" She kept on walking. Ungraceful and dignified, my father was like a pelican plodding behind. "Wait for me, Margarita!" he repeated.

I began shouting from the balcony, "Wait for Papa, wait!"

"Come, Marta. Call Ricardo. Today . . . Come!" she shouted, and, as she reached the house, she explained, "I've been rushing to talk to you and your brother. Take advantage of the beach this morning. We're leaving this afternoon!"

"Why, but why? We've been here only a week!" I demanded.

"Stop screaming, dear. Get your bathing suits, you and Ricardo, hurry!"

At the beach my father had begged my mother not to accept the repeated invitations from the local mayor's wife. The mayor was an unscrupulous man, and my father was intending to expose certain of his misdeeds. I was not to spend time at the beach with his daughters, either. Since it was going to be awkward to avoid their invitations and visits, the solution was to pack and return to the city. The thermometer of his principles, that ruler of our lives, was, as usual, interfering.

On my birthday last year, my father came home with a huge package and a bouquet of violets. Mama and I were on the sofa in the foyer. He put the package on my lap, then, bowing comically, almost to the ground, he offered me the bouquet.

The package contained a Spanish guitar.

With characteristic candor, Mama burst out, "Now, Marta, you won't mind staying home and playing your guitar."

The guitar was to replace my friends, who had nothing to do with me since my father was attacking the dictator daily in his editorials.

Now Ricardo comes back into the room, bringing a cake on a plate. In the center he has placed a stick with a piece of paper: "From Ricardo and Perico."

"A cake, a chocolate cake!" But as I take the plate, I see it's mud. My brother has shaped it into a perfect cake, imitating glossy chocolate frosting.

Papa and I laugh and joke about cutting ourselves large pieces.

Mama frowns. "I don't find it funny. Your sense of humor, Ricardo . . . frankly."

"It's a gift, Margarita. I mean Ricardo's cheerfulness," Papa protests, and, as often happens lately, his eyes glisten and his cheeks tremble slightly.

To change the subject, I speak about the rainy season. "At the market everyone says—" I realize that what I am going to say is the wrong thing to bring into our conversation, but it's too late. I finish my sentence. "They say that there will be scarcity of food."

"That there will be many Saturdays when the campesinos won't be able to come because of the bad roads," Ricardo adds.

"It'll be a good idea to build a stock of food, Margarita," Papa says. "It's fortunate," he goes on, "that the fruits and vegetables don't need refrigeration here. The weather permits piling food on the kitchen table, even the meat."

Mama, Ricardo, and I exchange glances. Bones to make soup are all we have been able to afford these past weeks.

My father doesn't realize that by now the cash we brought along is almost gone. He doesn't see that the weather, although damp, is not cold enough to keep away the ants against which Mama struggles at all hours. He, who knows the right words to say, understands little of realities.

My mother nods. Indeed, yes, we must get prepared for the rainy season. "Next Saturday I'll make a long list," she addresses my brother and me, then closes her eyes briefly. It's with us she shares the truth. Papa is now the child to be deceived.

In a moment Ricardo and I will go to the kitchen, where Papa will not see our lunch: watery vegetable soup and a piece of papaya.

Mama has stopped coming to sit by the window with me. She wants to avoid saying to me: "Soon there will be no reason for you and Ricardo to go to the market" and "To whom shall I write asking for a loan?" and "Should I send a note to the colonel, telling him we'll come to have our meals at the base mess hall, as was suggested at first?"

She makes no exception on my birthday—I sit by myself in front of the window.

Fernando is in the plaza. I begin dreaming, imagining that he and I are strolling in a park in the city . . . holding hands in a movie . . . reading poetry together. And yet sometimes I find myself thinking that the Fernando I see at the market has nothing to do with the one who circles the plaza, inspiring my fantasies.

I peek out the window. The soldier is taking his nap. My father and Ricardo are in their rooms, and Mama is in the backyard, washing.

Papa's cough is the only sound in the house as I tiptoe along the corridor to close the door of my room, to make Mama and Ricardo believe that I'm inside resting.

The guard is seated against the wall between the door and the window. Rifle across his legs, shoulders slumped, head twisted to one side, he looks like a marionette. He stirs as I step out, but I move quickly downhill.

So strong an impulse to meet must also be in Fernando's heart, the combination of our two forces, I tell myself. He must be waiting for me.

Three soldiers are in the parking lot, in front of the base building. One, facing the bottom of the hill where I am hesitating, suddenly ducks to the ground. They are playing *pompo,* a game with pebbles they use as dice.

I dash out of the fort and cross the road toward the narrow street that leads to the plaza. In a window a curtain moves, but I keep looking ahead, walking with confidence. Fernando, however, is not at the corner waiting for me as I had expected. I pause, my eyes searching. The sight of the empty plaza intimidates me suddenly. I was foolish to follow my impulse. I'm overcome by weakness at the prospect of walking all the way back by myself. I had counted on Fernando accompanying me up to the fort gate, confronting any soldiers who might appear. Just as I am about to leave, a shadow catches the corner of my eye. It's Fernando, on the side of the cantina.

We move toward one another but not across the plaza. I walk close to the little store and the closed doors and windows of the houses nearby. There's music from a radio inside one of the houses.

"This way," he whispers, tossing away the cigarette he has been smoking, and I turn the way I just came.

Is he taking me to his house? I won't go there. I ask and answer simultaneously.

We're going to a place nearby where we can sit and chat, he explains. "Nobody will see us there."

He's leading me to the path behind the church, the one we walk on every Sunday on our way to mass.

He saw me before I reached the corner, he says. "There was someone at the door of the store. I had to distract his attention away from you. I practically dragged the man inside the cantina, inviting him for a drink, hoping that you wouldn't leave in the meantime. Didn't you see him at the door of the store?"

"I didn't see anyone. Who was the man?"

"Pacho Arrieta, a pal of my uncle's." He waves to dismiss the subject.

A dog detaches itself from a doorway and follows us a few steps, barking, but there's no one around.

It's cold. I'm wearing a cotton blouse and my cardigan. Noticing that I'm trembling, Fernando takes off his coat and slips it over my shoulders.

We are sheltered by the weeping willows close to the stream with the wooden crosses alongside it. What a strange place to be, I say to myself. We step over the small puddles from last night's rain, then to a big stone surrounded by bushes and wildflowers, white and yellow daisies that give off a strong aroma. He spreads his handkerchief on the uneven surface so I can sit.

We don't speak for a moment while he keeps gazing at my face in a way that increases my uneasiness.

"I can't believe it's you here with me, Marta. I've waited for this to happen many times, and today when I saw you leaving the window I thought . . . I knew the moment had come at last!"

He puts his hands over mine, which are closed in fists on my lap. For a moment our hands move around each other's; then we lace our fingers.

"Why didn't you come to the market last Saturday?"

"Nobody woke me up, and Ricardo decided to go without me."

"I had something to tell you, old news by now. Bad news in any case."

"Something about your letter to the colonel? Did he answer?"

"He didn't bother to answer. Instead, he called my uncle and gave him my letter." He looks at me, expecting to see a disappointment I cannot pretend. I never believed I was going to be allowed to teach, and the prospect of working under Doña Paulina dampened my initial enthusiasm.

"There was an argument, a fight really, between my uncle and me. We insulted each other, and Mama and my sisters, they cried and went into hysterics. My mother, of course, had one of her rheumatism attacks."

"What did your uncle say?"

"It doesn't matter. He—my uncle, well, he thinks I am—that the letter was risking our position, that Colonel Ferreira may use it as a pretext to give our jobs to someone else, and that we could lose our house. The house, of course, is what matters, but let's not waste time with all that, Marta."

"All because of me, Fernando. I'm sorry."

"Forget it, please. What I was hoping was that we would see each other every day. . . . I had so many dreams,

124

Marta. And now I don't want to be here any longer."

"Yes, go away, Fernando. You shouldn't waste your years in this pueblo; you must go to the city, find a life for yourself there." I even tell him the little phrase that so often comes to my mind when I'm looking at him from the window: "You are also a prisoner in this pueblo."

Fernando raises his eyebrows, somewhat puzzled by my long recital. "Marta, listen. You don't understand. I want to go away with you!" He clutches me in his arms. "At three o'clock there's a bus to Marañón. We'll walk a mile or so to catch it in a spot where no one from around here will see us. My aunt Blanca, she's very fond of me. She lives in Marañón, and she'll help us." His mouth is behind my ear. His last words come out unclear. I realize that a lock of my hair is filling his mouth. He kisses my lips, then my throat. "Don't you want me like I want you, Marta, *mi amor?*"

"Let's run away, yes, Fernando!" I burst out.

His coat slips off my shoulders, his hat flies away, falling behind the stone. We stumble to the ground, grabbing at each other.

There is a softness under me, like a mattress, a cold mattress, but his hands are warm on my flesh, moving under my blouse, over my breasts, then rolling down my panties.

The frogs that were silent are now croaking wildly in the stream. And then I hear a soft whistle and approaching steps.

"What's that?"

Fernando quickly covers my mouth with his hand. Immobile, we soothe our terror against each other.

A campesino and his donkey are trotting along the path, parallel to where we are. He whacks the animal's rump with a stick. His woman is at his heels and, whistling behind, a boy throws stones into the puddles.

"Damn campesinos!" Fernando says, and we sigh with relief.

His hand is darkened with mud. I feel mud also between my lips where he pressed his hand to keep me quiet. Now I recognize the feeling of the cold mattress under me. It's the sodden ground, cloaked by the bushes.

"My God!" I cry out, but Fernando, unaware, kisses my ears, trying to recapture the interrupted mood.

"Let's run away," he begins anew.

I push him away.

". . . Marañón . . . We'll write our families. I love you."

"Please! We're lying in a mudhole!" I say.

Fernando sees at last and, with the back of his hand, he begins wiping my face, looking at himself. "My God!" It's he who now exclaims, scrambling to his feet to fetch his coat and hat.

Nearby, my pink panties look like an overgrown flower floating on the bushes. My wet skirt sticks to the backs of my legs. "What am I going to do?" I repeat over and over.

His sister Cecilia will lend me clothes, he says. "We can go by my house and sneak into my room, where you can change." One sleeve of his white shirt is black with dirt.

We look at each other. A streak of mud crosses his face from cheek to cheek and over his nose. For an instant I want to laugh at the absurdity of our situation. The back of my head is soaked with mud.

"I should have known better. This cursed place, last night's rain. It's my fault, Marta." His face is all sadness. I wonder if there is ever humor or mischief or rebellion in his handsome face. I yearn to feel as I did a moment ago, to hold his mud-smeared face in my hands. But, like so many times, I am thinking: This Fernando standing in front of me—does he have anything to do with the one I dream about by the window? I look away.

"What am I going to do?" The thought of facing my family with my drenched, muddy clothes fills my mind.

"Come," he says, and I follow him to the stream.

The bank sinks under our feet.

"Wait here, Marta."

He leaps to a stone. Crouching, he washes his handkerchief and hands it to me. I wipe my face, my ears, suddenly remembering my mother's gift. I press both hands against my earrings. He continues rinsing the handkerchief and passing it to me. I rub at my blouse and skirt, but there's little I can do to improve my appearance.

"It's getting late; we'd better go now, Fernando."

"We'll go back along this path. No one will see us."

We step out of the weeping willows' shelter.

"After we cross the main road, we'll go to the left of the fort and around to the back entrance. There you'll be able to climb to your house through the base yard."

"But they'll see me, Fernando, the men from the base. There are always soldiers and officers around the yard."

"Let me think." He looks in the direction of the plaza. "Look, Marta, it'll be worse to return through the plaza. Even though there usually aren't any people around, women are always peeking from behind windows, and this man, this Pacho Arrieta, my uncle's friend, he may still be roaming about. I hardly know the man, and there I was, suddenly inviting him for a drink and then leaving him alone. He would be thrilled to see us and have something to report to my uncle."

We both keep looking right and left, trying to decide which way to go. He fumbles in his pocket and pulls out a cigarette. The match struggles with the wind for a moment.

"This way!" He takes my hand, and we start along the path that will put us at the back entrance of the fort.

We walk for a while without speaking. The air feels as if rain will start pouring any moment. The wetness of my clothes creeps through me.

Unexpectedly, he puts his arm around my shoulders. "We still have time, you know . . . to catch the bus."

I say nothing as he goes on insisting, repeating, "Let's run away, Marta."

Finally I say, "You're asking me to leave my family, my sick father. I can't do that, Fernando."

"But a moment ago you talked of going away with me." The cigarette in the corner of his mouth balances as he speaks.

"A moment ago neither you nor I was thinking. I can't leave my family . . . our circumstances, you understand." I stop abruptly. "Fernando, I need your help!" And words I haven't planned to say begin coming out of me. "Could you go to the city this weekend? I'll give you Doctor Camacho's address. It would involve no risk, no risk at all, Fernando. Camacho is not mixed up in any struggle against the government. All you'll have to do is to deliver a letter."

His grip on my shoulder eases.

Something within me relaxes, as though my asking Fernando's help for my father justifies our rendezvous by the stream.

As we walk on, I wait for his answer. He shakes his head slightly.

"All I'm asking is for you to deliver a letter. If there's a package to bring, it would be something small that would probably fit in one of your pockets."

But Fernando, still shaking his head, says nothing.

"A jar of capsules for my father, that would be it. . . . And you said you love me, Fernando."

128

"You can't make me the target for your father's enemies. I have an invalid mother and sisters who depend on me. Your father isn't the only person who matters, Marta!"

There are steps behind us. We stop and hesitate while searching for a tree or someplace to hide.

"It's all right; keep walking," Fernando says.

Two campesinos are approaching behind us. *"Buenas tardes,"* they greet us. One carries a heavy load on his back tied to a leather strap across his forehead. They pass us running in a mulelike trotting step.

Fernando is sulking like a little boy, his lower lip thrust out.

"Sorry, Marta, I won't be your messenger," he says after a moment. "But one thing I will do. I'll leave this horrid place!"

"Good, Fernando. I mean I'm glad that you're going away," I say with sincerity. "If your decision has something to do with me, then I'm glad."

"I have been your toy," he says melodramatically. "Whatever attention you have given me was only because you expected me to help you with your father . . . your father!"

I want to say something, but nothing comes to my mind except "I'm sorry, Fernando."

It's beginning to sprinkle. We are nearing the main road. There's the *brrrr* of an engine advancing, then a shadow wavering on the road like a drunkard.

"The bus to Marañón," Fernando says softly.

Such is my panic at the prospect of facing my family that I am tempted to say, "Let's wait for the bus." We cross the road rapidly.

To our right is the hill with our house at the top.

"There, look!" someone shouts.

I draw closer to Fernando. "Did you hear? Who's that?"

We both turn. A soldier is behind us; other men are com-

129

ing along the little street we take when we go to the market. We can hear voices.

"It's soldiers, I'm sure. Come!" But I sense his uneasiness as we both increase our pace. We skirt the wall that encloses the fort and hurry toward the back entrance. A soldier is stationed at the gate.

"It looks like the rains are already with us," Fernando says, pushing me ahead of him, trying to engage the soldier in conversation. The man salutes, saying, "Señor Profesor," and gives me a side-glance, mumbling something.

"It's all right," Fernando says. As I move ahead, I hear him offering the soldier a cigarette.

Between the wall that encloses the fort and the soldiers' barracks and latrines there are piles of garbage, among them empty wooden cases of whiskey and American canned foods.

I walk along the long passage that leads to the yard of the base and to the embankment that separates the military quarters from our backyard. I pray that my mother isn't there washing clothes.

I'll have to face the soldiers in the yard alone, I am saying to myself. But the voices I hear are behind me, the shuffling of feet as well.

I run and begin scrambling up the embankment. Someone grips my hand. "Ouch! You're hurting me!" I turn, expecting it to be Fernando. Instead, I see a man I recognize immediately. He is the mayor's friend, always with him at the market.

He pulls me down forcefully. I half fall as I slide down the embankment backward. Then, yanking my arm, he turns me around. "Watch!"

Below, near the flagpole, in the center of the yard, is Fernando, surrounded by the mayor, an officer, and two soldiers. His face is ashen, his tie twisted, and his hat lies on the ground. The figures move around Fernando, each one taking a place, as though in a familiar ritual where everyone knows his role. They are going to execute Fernando! He first, then . . . me, I say to myself.

The soldiers pin his arms behind him. The mayor begins slapping Fernando in the face.

"*Mire,* watch!" the man shouts, pulling and hurting my hand.

Fernando's head bounces from side to side as the mayor continues hitting it, hitting it like a punching bag.

". . . ruin . . . your mother . . . sisters!" The mayor roars the words. Stopping at last, the mayor looks up at the embankment. "*Vamos,* Pacho!" he calls to his friend. Then, shaking his index finger, he yells something else, looking at me. I understand one word—*lesson.*

Pacho lifts my hand for a moment, then drops it and rushes down the embankment.

Fernando staggers toward the flagpole. Although his face is turned away, I can see he has covered his nose and mouth with his handkerchief.

One of the soldiers who pinned his arms picks up the hat from the ground and offers it to Fernando courteously.

The words of the mayor suddenly become clear, as if the threat has been traveling through the air, reaching me only now, "Lesson number one!"

The mayor pats the officer's shoulder while the mayor, in turn, is being patted on the back by his friend Pacho, the three marching across the yard into the base.

I cannot move. Such is the shaking that seizes me, I feel my legs giving out from under me. Scattered over the base yard I see several still figures, like statues, their heads lifted up to the embankment—the soldiers staring at me.

At last I manage to turn and begin climbing.

🌀 17

Rain falls incessantly. Some days it's only a drizzle that goes on and on. I prefer it when it falls hard, drumming on the roof, splashing on the yard's puddles, pounding the broken bottles that top the wall. Then something releases within me, as if the rain is shouting my despair.

Two weeks have gone by since my meeting with Fernando.

Mother was not in the yard when I arrived. By then, however, my muddied clothes had become insignificant in contrast with the terror I was feeling, which stayed with me for several days.

Was Fernando subjected to further humiliation? Did he leave? I exposed him to the cruelty of his uncle. But my concern for Fernando is artificial, something I force into my mind. It's my safety and my family's that fills my thoughts constantly.

Ricardo has been going to the market without me. It doesn't take him long to come back with a light basket containing a few vegetables and fruits and the bones to make soup.

My father seldom leaves his bedroom, and Mama spends much time with him.

This morning something different is taking place. Mama and my father are in the living room with the door closed.

One moment we hear their low voices; the next, the Remington.

Ricardo and I look at each other with expectancy. Anything, even the failure of whatever they are planning, is preferable to the passivity with which we daily accept our fate.

The guard who stands by our door is in the entrance hall. He is there most of the time now to protect himself from the rain. Last night he came into the house.

Mama went to him immediately. "Please remain in the entrance hall. My husband needs total silence. Here, take this blanket, and there's the straw mat by the door. Don't come into the house!"

Something about my mother inspired submissiveness from the guard. *"Sí, señora,"* he answered, and *"Perdón,"* and *"Gracias."*

Saturday nights Pedro also comes into the entrance hall— rain has been no obstacle to the drunken fiestas at the base. He and my brother play the game *pompo,* with pebbles replacing dice.

Mama then asks Pedro to come into the living room briefly to have a cup of consommé she reserves for him. We talk uninterruptedly, Mama and I, while he sips, to avoid his blunt campesino remarks about my father's appearance. "Don Miguel, *pobrecito,* he looks like an apparition."

Last Saturday we overheard what he said to Ricardo in the entrance hall: "A crow is always perched on the roof of this house. I don't like it. Death and crows walk together."

"You talk too much, Pedrito. Come on, play!"

At last the door opens. Mama asks us to come in. Bent over the Remington, my father is reading a paper.

"Your father has written a letter to Felipe Barrera; you remember him. He was once a close friend; now he has a high position in the government," Mama explains.

My father lifts the paper; then, as if dismayed by the effort of reading, he lowers his arm wearily. "You read it, Margarita."

Dear Felipe,

Encouraged by sentiments of our old friendship, I do not hesitate to ask you to intercede for the freedom of my two children. It is Margarita's and my hope that Marta and Ricardo will be allowed to return to the city, where they will reside at the house of their uncle, Alberto Arenas, and his family. The impact of this isolation on our children, to mention only one factor, is of deep concern to us.

We trust in the effectiveness of your intervention, for which we thank you in advance.

No one speaks for a moment. Then I say, "I won't go back to the city, leaving the two of you here." I am aware that my words are mostly dictated by my lack of faith in the letter.

"To have the two of you free in the city will improve your father's health. As things are now, he's not fighting his sickness."

"I should have thought of writing this letter before. I'm sorry. It was your mother's idea," my father says.

"Don't send it, Papa. Marta and I won't leave the two of you here."

"It's not only your freedom, Ricardo," my father answers. "You'll be able to send us medicines and money. You see, the rent . . ." He glances at Mama.

She continues. "The rent from the newspaper building should now amount to a substantial sum. You'll be able to help, to do something in the city."

"But they won't give you our letters or the medicines or

the money," Ricardo puts in. "Isn't that what you're always saying, Mama, that they keep our mail at the base?"

My father comments that he doesn't believe there has been mail for us. "I honestly feel that no one has attempted to get in touch with us. They're afraid."

Mama folds the letter carefully, puts it in the addressed envelope, and she herself goes to the entrance hall to give it to the soldier.

We listen to the guard explaining that he cannot leave his post but that his replacement will be coming at any moment. "And then I'll give your letter to the colonel."

Back in the room, Mama says that she has faith in the letter. "Everything will work out. We did the right thing, Miguel."

"Barrera will try. One way or another, we'll hear from him, I know. It's because of Felipe's influence that I am still . . ."

"Barrera is a good man," Mama adds, and the two go on reassuring each other of the success of the letter.

"But will the colonel send it?"

"He will, Ricardo! The colonel would not dare to keep a letter addressed to someone of Barrera's importance. He is—what's his position, Miguel?"

"Minister of Internal Affairs."

Our mood has improved since the letter was written. Mother's soups taste better, and Ricardo is again trying to make us laugh. "Look, I caught a fish," he says, showing a shred of meat from the soup bone.

"To go to sleep with a light stomach is good for the digestion," Mama repeats. "As long as we have carrots and bananas—they're loaded with vitamins." From the hostess of a pension she has turned into a dietician, pointing out to

Ricardo and me the nutritional value of the yucca and the carrots she gives us daily.

Ricardo and I now have something to speak about. Mostly my brother talks about food. Aunt Lila's Sunday luncheons and her famous lamb stew, and the dishes that our maid, Ana, who is now at their house, will prepare for us.

I think about my room, my books, my guitar. I long with an almost physical ache for every corner of our home. Each moment I find myself listening for the footsteps of the soldier coming into the house to deliver Barrera's answer to my father's letter. And my brother's voice in the background goes on, "Cheese . . . crackers . . . ice cream."

Then abruptly we stop, remorseful at our readiness to leave our parents.

"Marta, Marta." My mother switches on the ceiling bulb in my room.

I turn my head to the wall and cover my face with the blanket.

"I want to talk to you." She strokes my shoulder and sits on the edge of my cot. "Listen, Marta. I need your help. We have to take some action. We can't remain with folded arms while your father is dying."

I sit up, fully awake.

It's raining, and there is lightning and thunder like almost every night. Papa's cough, however, can be heard distinctly.

"I wrote to Dr. Camacho and Alberto; I wrote to Juan Hernández. Pedro assured Ricardo that he gave the letters to a friend of his, a truck driver who travels back and forth to the city, and, you see, no answers."

"When did you send the letters, Mama?"

"Five weeks ago. Pedro says he won't risk himself again, and of course we shouldn't expose the soldier. . . . Listen,

Marta, I've been thinking about this Fernando, your friend. Could you get him to help us?"

"I don't believe he's in the pueblo anymore. We'll have to think of something else."

"What about his sisters? There must be a way to ask for their help. And his invalid mother, she'd understand."

"She'd understand nothing, Mama. Fernando's mother is the mayor's sister."

"What? Sister, mayor," Mama mumbles. "Your friend's mother? But why? I mean, you didn't mention anything about this before." The weak bulb of the ceiling accentuates her pallor. She's wearing her cardigan over her robe.

We don't speak for a moment. Then Mama says, "I woke you up to tell you a decision I just made. Tomorrow I'll go speak to Colonel Ferreira. Don't interrupt me." She puts out her hand. "We have to get your father into a hospital. I'll ask the colonel to allow me to call Dr. Camacho on their telephone. Ricardo will come with me, and you'll stay here with your father. I've made up my mind. Tomorrow!"

Her eyes are intent on my face. She longs to hear my approval. Why is my mother so naïve? I am wondering. Has she forgotten what she said to me the first day we learned there was no doctor or medicines for my father in this pueblo: "The General must be pleased. Your father is providing a variation to his killing methods." Colonel Ferreira will be quick to report that the dictator's sentence is being carried out.

She still waits for me to say something while she goes on twisting the buttons of her sweater.

It occurs to me that I'm seeing Mama's true expression for the first time, that the invisible wires holding her features in the restrained countenance she showed a moment ago have all snapped. I look away from the fear and desolation of that face. I want to comfort my mother, to rock her in my arms as if she were my child.

"I talked to Ricardo a moment ago. He's all upset because I'm going to see the colonel."

"Let's wait a few days, Mama. Papa said that Barrera will answer one way or another. Maybe we'll hear this week."

"Maybe . . . maybe! We can't waste more time making conjectures, Marta. These past few days your father has been giving me instructions about our future as if . . . You've heard him."

We have heard the weak but persistent voice of my father at all hours, explaining that the mortgage on our house has been paid, that the rent from the newspaper building is waiting, that our lawyer collects from the small coffee farm. At all hours my father has been repeating, "Are you listening, Margarita?" and "Don't interrupt me, Margarita."

"I'm sorry I woke you up," Mama is saying. "Go back to sleep now." She turns off the ceiling bulb. "It'll be all right tomorrow, Marta," she says from the door. A flash of lightning illuminates her silhouette.

⌐ 18

I tell myself that last night's conversation with my mother did not take place. It was a dream.

But I notice that she has planned the day differently. At siesta hour she doesn't disappear into the backyard to wash clothes, but rather reads to my father in his room.

Ricardo and I are in the kitchen having lunch. We don't speak as we eat our plain rice and a banana. My brother keeps looking down at his hands. His nails are bitten to the quick, and the fingertips look red and sore.

We can hear Mama's thin, strained voice as she reads *Don Quixote* to our father. She doesn't pause when he coughs. Her voice rises a note higher, accelerating.

Calculating that the colonel is up from his siesta, she comes out, makes a sign to Ricardo from the corridor, and returns to the bedroom.

After a moment she tiptoes out, carrying her purse and high-heeled shoes under her blazer. Her hair is set in a high chignon. She's wearing her dark blue suit.

Presently Ricardo comes out of his room. He's dressed in his best suit, which he has outgrown.

"Marta, be alert in case your father calls me," she says softly.

I follow them to the entrance hall, where the soldier is lying on the straw mat, napping.

He scrambles to his feet. "Where are you—you can't leave the house, señora!"

"We're going to see Colonel Ferreira!" Mama says curtly and keeps moving. The guard picks up his rifle, walks behind my mother and Ricardo a few steps, then returns to stand by the door, muttering under his breath.

I rush to the living room window to watch my mother and Ricardo.

It's drizzling. There are puddles everywhere, but the soldiers have placed boards, like a bridge, along the path from our house down to the base building.

My mother moves awkwardly, her heels digging into the mud in the gaps between the boards. Holding her arm, my brother is pathetic in his shrunken suit. I remain at the window until they disappear into the base.

The stillness of the house is interrupted only by my father's cough. After a moment he calls, "Marta, Ricardo."

Odd that he's not calling my mother as he always does. I wait.

"Marta, are you there . . . or is it you, Ricardo?"

I go to him. Pushing open the bedroom door, which is already ajar, I ask if there's something I can do. He doesn't answer. "Try to rest, Papa."

As I am halfway back to the living room, his voice returns: "Marta! Don't you hear me?"

I walk into the room that my brother and I are not supposed to enter. It's dark inside, but I can see he's lying faceup on his cot. There's a pungent smell of alcohol and garlic. Mama has been mashing garlic and giving it to him, a peasant medicine for the cough, a medicine that she used to mock.

He points to a pile of rags in a paper sack by the side of

the cot. I hand him one and stand there while he coughs, covering his mouth with the rag. In the semidarkness I see a stain of blood like a map on the white cloth. He folds the rag quickly to hide it from me and keeps it in his hand, which hangs outside the cot. I pretend I have seen nothing. I look at the crucifix on the wall above him with Mama's silver rosary around it, then at *Don Quixote* and *Cortizos' Easy Guide to Learning English,* and finally at the rag in his hand, which I am afraid to touch. I notice a pail with crumpled rags in the corner.

My mother has torn one of the sheets to make scarf-size handkerchiefs. She washes the rags separately from the other clothes. I have never asked about the oversized handkerchiefs for fear of learning what I now know.

At last my hand moves to take away the cloth, hot with my father's blood. I throw it in the pail with the soiled rags; then I sit in Mama's chair by the cot.

"Marta."

"Yes, Papa," I say, trying to sound casual.

"Your mother, is Ricardo with her?"

"Ricardo?" I shout, overacting my surprise. Does he suspect that Mama and Ricardo have gone somewhere?

"Ricardo—I think he's with Perico."

He closes his eyes. I watch the blanket moving evenly up and down. After a moment I start to leave.

He turns to me, while shaking his hand toward the night table.

"Do you want me to read something to you, Papa?"

"Alcohol, your hands! Don't you know any better?" he says severely.

I take the bottle and clumsily pour alcohol over my hands, spilling some on my skirt and legs. I am crying softly, trying to conceal my face, but my sniffles fill the room.

"Don't be afraid, Marta."

I think of a night long ago when I was a child. There was a moving shadow near my window. I jumped out of bed and dashed downstairs to Papa's study, where he was still typing. "I'm scared, Papa." Holding hands, we climbed back to my room. "It's the almond tree, see, Marta? The shadow of the branches swaying in the wind. Don't be afraid. I'll read by your door." I remember how he whispered what he was reading to reassure me that he was there watching. I went back to sleep, lulled by the murmur of his voice.

"The three of you . . . my fault," he murmurs now.

It doesn't matter that I'm not grasping every word he's saying. The whole room seems impregnated with what I have often seen in the small, cloudy eyes of my father when he looks at Mama, Ricardo, and me: "I have inflicted this on you. . . . *Mea culpa, mea culpa.*"

"It's all right, Papa," I go on repeating. There must be something else, other words to comfort my father, but my mind is blank as I keep saying the meaningless phrase, "It's all right, Papa."

After a moment he closes his eyes and thanks me for coming in. "I must obey your mother; I'll rest now."

I return to the window. It seems a long time since Mama and Ricardo left the house.

Our guard moves in front of the window, looking at me with curiosity.

At last I see Ricardo, then Mama, coming from the base. Moving ahead of her, my brother keeps snatching leaves from the bushes along the path. From the window I can sense his frustration. Following him, my mother is a lonely figure trudging against the wind.

I wait for them at the entrance hall. "What took you so long? Did you speak to the colonel?"

"They made us wait," Mama says, taking off her muddy shoes.

"What did he say?"

"He said—" but she interrupts herself. "Ricardo will tell you." She looks exhausted. Did my father call while she was gone? she wants to know.

"Everything was fine, Mama." Before I finish saying it, she's in his room.

I knock on Ricardo's door.

He's changing his clothes, he says. After a moment he asks me in. He's lying on the cot, one arm across his forehead.

"I want to know what happened. Please tell me, Ricardo."

"We should never have gone! Mama—you should have seen her. She was touching the colonel's hand, his sleeve, pleading, *'Por favor, por favor,'* and he kept saying, 'Yes, señora, of course, a doctor for Don Miguel.' He won't send anyone, of course, and is probably laughing with the others." Without a pause, Ricardo goes on, "And Papa's friend, Barrera, he's dead. The army plane he was traveling in crashed in the Amazon jungle. 'Ah, yes, señora, a great loss,' the stupid man kept saying. The General probably sent Barrera on the mission to be killed. As if this doesn't happen all the time. The letter was never sent. The colonel gave it back to Mama."

I sit on the cot.

"Mama wasn't allowed to call Dr. Camacho. The colonel said that their telephone is a party line to be used only for military matters. But Mama, she still went on. She asked if you and I could have our meals at the base as they had suggested the day we arrived."

"And?"

"The colonel said that he would have to write headquar-

143

ters for authorization and that the answer may take weeks to arrive."

We are both quiet for a while.

"We should never have gone! There's something I want to—"

"Don't tell me any more. I don't want to hear it!"

"It's about Papa, Marta. We can't let him find out about Barrera. We should go on pretending that we're optimistic, waiting for his answer, that we haven't lost hope."

I look at my brother. He is wise and generous. He would have found words to comfort Papa in his bedroom. I am older, but I don't know. I still don't know what was the right thing to have said to my father.

🔲 19

"Here, Marta, for the aspirins and the alcohol. And see what you can bring with the change."

I look at the two peso bills and the twenty-centavo coin in my hand. "What can I . . ." I begin, but Mama has already walked out of my room.

Ricardo cannot go to the market. He has boils on his legs. Mama keeps bathing them with hot water and mint leaves.

Polo is waiting at the door. I haven't been out of the house since the day of my meeting with Fernando. It's not raining this morning. As I move downhill, I feel a lightness, a desire to run and to smile. It's the feeling of freedom and being away from the sound of my father's cough.

The roads are flooded, Polo says, and only the ones who traveled with their burros will be at the plaza. "You don't look—you're not like you used to look, señorita."

"I'm skinny and ugly," I mutter softly.

"What?"

"I'm fine. It's Ricardo who's not well. He has boils."

"He's hungry; that's what's the matter with him." Last time he escorted my brother to the market, the soldier goes on, he could see that Ricardo wanted to eat everything in sight. "His eyes were the size of a full moon, looking at the fruits and the sweets. And that was two weeks ago!"

Two weeks ago Mama went to see the colonel. Or was it three weeks ago? I have lost my sense of time. Weekends alone remain identifiable through the ringing of the church bells and the exploding of the firecrackers. We've stopped going to mass on Sundays. "We must pray here at home," Mama says. "We can't leave your father alone."

"My brothers and sisters, we all used to get the boils like your brother's," Polo says.

"But you had fruits and eggs and corn. Didn't you say you come from a mountain nearby? You lived on a farm, didn't you?"

"We lived in a hut on the hacienda of Don Cristobal Porras. Everything belonged to him. If my mother and my older brothers and sisters didn't sell at the market and bring back the money, then the *patrón* threatened to throw us out and give our hut to somebody else. We got only the overripe fruit and the sick chickens, things that couldn't sell at the market. But corn we had, yes; we ate *mazamorra* every day. Don Cristobal was good. He gave us eight or ten pesos every month, depending on what we sold at the market. They flew away like the wind, the pesos."

"Is your family still—"

"My mother died long ago, and my brothers and sisters, they're scattered all over. I'm the youngest."

I sense a difference in the soldier. His voice is conversational, soft, as if he were speaking to someone close to him, with whom he doesn't have to pretend, as if suddenly I am not the señorita from the city, but someone who knows poverty, the poverty with which he has been familiar all his life.

We are now in the plaza.

"Look, didn't I tell you? Only a few are here to sell." He points to a group of campesinos who are gathered in the center of the plaza under a tarpaulin roof held up with poles.

"When you had plenty, that time when you came bringing rolls of pesos, I kept telling you and your brother to save for the rainy season, like the rest of the people, but you didn't believe me. Are they all gone, the pesos?"

"What happens, Polo, is that we—" I begin speaking without knowing what I am going to say next. "We are supposed to receive some money from the city, but it hasn't come yet, you see? So today I'll have to buy on credit."

"Credit? You mean you're not going to pay for what you get, what we call around here *fiado*?"

I nod.

"You'll get nothing that way, señorita. People are more poor in the rainy season; you'll get *nada,* I tell you!" As he speaks he hurries on, animated at the prospect of proving himself right.

I am pleased to notice that the campesina from whom we often buy is among the few who are here today.

She greets me cordially. "What happened, señorita? You're all bones like the boy, your brother; he don't look good neither."

"It's the climate; we're not accustomed to it."

Polo, by my side, is alert to every word I say.

I wait for a local woman and her daughter to get the change that the campesina is counting out to them. Then she wraps a few wrinkled pesos and coins into a red-flowered bandanna and pushes it down inside her blouse.

The local woman and the girl leave, each carrying a loaded basket.

I drop one knee to the ground and thrust my face close

to the campesina, who sits on a wooden box. I begin babbling my invented speech about the money we are expecting from the city. "It will be here soon—"

"What's that you saying, señorita? I can't hear you," shrieks the campesina.

Several heads turn in our direction.

In confusion I grab a papaya and place it at the bottom of the basket, then a bunch of bananas, a pineapple, carrots, potatoes, yucca. I can't stop myself. I probe the tomatoes, the oranges, and add a handful of parsley and several eggs.

Polo, one knee on the ground also, has his mouth half-open as he looks on.

My basket is full, looking like a picture. The red and yellow and green colors alternating, and at the top, the parsley is a nest for the eggs. I admire my arrangement while wondering why, before, I had not been aware of the beautiful shapes and textures of fruits and vegetables.

"And the plums, señorita!" The campesina selects a few, rubbing each one against her bosom until the red, smooth skin of the fruit shines "like them cheeks of the holy angels."

"How much?" I ask. Out of the corner of my eye, I see Polo's mouth dropping an extra inch.

"Let me see, señorita." She moves the eggs to one side of the basket tenderly, digging both hands in to feel what is at the bottom. Then she begins her complicated arithmetic, adding with her fingers, calling each item in diminutive, in the peasant manner, "The big *papayita,* and the juicy *naranjitas* . . . Let me see." She goes on and on.

As I hear the pounding of my heart, I am tempted to grab the basket and run like a thief.

"Thirteen pesitos and forty . . . forty-two, forty-five . . . fifty centavos, that's all for all that. I sell you cheap, señorita."

"You're very good to me, thank you!" Getting to my feet,

catching my breath, I add, "I'll pay you next time. I have only two pesos today, but the money will come soon. I'll pay you later."

The campesina grunts, scowls, and stares at me as if I've spoken in a foreign tongue. "What's that you say?" Her eyes shift from me to Polo.

"She'll pay you some other time," Polo says. "She has no pesos; she's poor like you and me; her brother has the boils."

"Polo!" I cry out, feeling the blood rushing to my face.

The woman looks at my blouse and my cardigan, which are discolored, then at my skirt and loafers, which are shabby, but to her they are luxurious. Her beady eyes squint with resentment.

"You know me well; you're my friend," I say.

Her mouth twists in an ugly grimace. "Your *amiga*?" And she chuckles with an irony that seems odd for so simple a woman. "You're a señorita and I'm a humble campesina. You're not my friend!" She pulls the basket toward her fiercely. "Some things you take; some things you don't. I need the pesos!"

Her hands are claws moving over the basket. First she takes out the eggs, leaving the parsley, then, one by one, the plums. Her hands keep digging, bringing out one, two, three tomatoes and the pineapple, but she leaves the rest.

"*Gracias.*" I give her a one-peso bill.

"One?" She turns the bill back and forth. "You said you had two pesos. Look, *mi Capitán*"—she shows the peso to Polo—"one miserable peso for all that!" She plunges forward to pull the basket again, but Polo lifts it quickly and walks away.

"*Gracias*, I'm sorry that—I'll pay you." I reach to touch her hand, which she snatches away, grumbling under her breath.

Polo, a few feet away, is waiting.

I am panting with shame. My throat is dry, and I grasp an orange from the basket, peel it, and start eating, unmindful of the soldier, who doesn't take his eyes off me.

In front of me two women halt. They sway to right and left; their feet shuffle—they are like two dancers who have forgotten their step. They are Elisa and Cecilia. Their eyes, larger than usual, look at me askance.

"*Hola,*" I call in a friendly way. Drawing closer to each other, they turn their backs and trip away quickly.

My ghostlike appearance startled them, and I know, of course, they want nothing to do with me. I stand there for a moment with half the orange in my hand.

"The Señor Profesor, he's gone, you know," Polo says.

"Gone? Oh, no! You mean he's dead?"

"Dead? Why do you say that? He's not dead. He's in a more important school, in Marañón. His uncle fixed it for him, the mayor. You know, after that day that you and he— you know that day—"

"Yes, Polo!"

The mayor's beating of his nephew because he was with me must still be the gossip of the village. I am relieved I did not think about this earlier, even more relieved that Elisa and Cecilia were not around when I didn't pay the campesina. There is always something to be thankful for.

"They have another professor now, an older señor, a widower. He is the uncle of the colonel's wife, and—"

" 'And they all lived happily ever after.' "

"Uh?"

"Polo, what's the name of the owner of the little store?"

"Don Nicanor." The soldier stops abruptly. "Oh, no, señorita. Are you going to buy without money from Don Nicanor also? I'll wait for you outside the store!"

Three tiny men with large felt hats and black ponchos are drinking rum, filling the little store that is already crammed with barrels of flour, beans, rice, and other grains. There is a smell of fried onions and wet wool.

"Good morning, señorita." Don Nicanor greets me with a smile. As usual, he's wearing a neat, open-necked khaki shirt under his poncho.

He doesn't see much of me these days, he says. Is it the weather that keeps me indoors? "There was sure some miscalculation when the good Lord gave us this climate!"

Dreading that he might say that I look skinny and pale, I grin widely, saying yes, the terrible weather, blinking with absurd animation.

"The rains are a curse on us, the poor!"

Polo did not stay out, as he had said. Standing near me, he's all ears.

"Don Nicanor," I whisper. I clear my throat, as if to muster my courage. "Don Nicanor, I have a favor to ask you."

One of the men turns his head, but I go on, "My family is expecting money from the city; it should be here—"

Before I finish, Don Nicanor's eyes are warm with understanding.

"*Tranquila, señorita.* The usual?"

"Please."

He moves to the shelf labeled MEDICAMENTOS, under a picture of Jesus adorned with red paper carnations. Thrusting his hand into a wide-mouthed flask, he returns to the counter, his cupped hands filled with aspirin envelopes. He picks up a large bottle of rubbing alcohol and sets it on the counter. "I'll be out in a minute," he says, going to the back of the store to the refrigerator to get the soup bones.

He returns with a larger package than I expected.

151

Polo takes it and puts it in the basket along with the alcohol and the aspirins, then steps out.

"Don Nicanor, one day I hope we can—" I begin, but my voice quivers and a tear, like an ant, crawls down my cheek.

"Anything else, señorita?"

I want to say "Rice, sugar, coffee."

"That's all, thank you, Don Nicanor."

As I am about to leave, he calls, "Señorita, you forgot something." He pushes toward me the one-peso bill and the twenty-cent coin I had left for him on the counter.

"But, Don Nicanor—"

"Please, señorita. You'll take care of this later, at your convenience," he says softly, walking away, pretending he's busy with the three men.

The prospect of going home with the large bottle of alcohol and the aspirins, with the bones for the soup and the half-filled basket plus one peso and the coin, fills me with sudden energy.

"Time to go home, Polo!"

He rushes to my side and gives me a piece of anise-flavored hard candy. I bite on it as we move away from the plaza. Then I realize that the soldier bought the sweet outside Don Nicanor's store from a stand teeming with flies. I want to spit. Instead, I push the piece I still have in my hand quickly into my mouth.

●

回 20

An officer is standing between the entrance hall and the living room—he has a black valise in his hand.

Mama, Ricardo, and I are seated around the kitchen table. We have been arguing, my brother and I, and he's crying.

"Good afternoon," the officer is saying. "I was told someone here needs a doctor."

My mother stands up. "A doctor—you are the doctor!" She rushes along the corridor, her hand extended toward the officer.

"It's your husband who is sick, isn't it?" He looks up and down at the thin, pale woman advancing toward him. "I'm Arturo Martínez."

"Here, Doctor Martínez, please. My husband is in here." She draws closer to the bedroom door, which is ajar.

The doctor glances at the puddles in the yard, the wall topped with broken bottles, the peeling doors, and down at the weeds between the bricks, like a house inspector taking inventory.

"Damp," he says softly, as though speaking to himself, "very damp."

"Please come in, Doctor. I didn't think—it was so long ago that my son and I went to see Colonel Ferreira. I'm glad you're here, Doctor Martínez!"

153

He explains that he's a visiting doctor, and his post is in an army hospital in a city to the south of us. "I was on an emergency call, but rain has made the roads impassable. I was forced to come this way, and Colonel Ferreira asked me to take a look at your husband."

Mama walks into the bedroom, the doctor following.

In reaction to the doctor's presence in our father's room, Ricardo and I begin laughing. It's a tittering laughter; then we start shrieking. Covering our mouths, we tiptoe along the corridor to be closer to the bedroom.

"It's dark in here," the doctor says.

"It's because the day is gray and the window is tiny and of course the weak ceiling bulb doesn't help," Mama apologizes, as if this is our home.

"It's all right, señora," the doctor interrupts. He has a flashlight in his valise, he says.

"*Buenos días, Señor Maldonado,* how are you today?" he calls in the booming voice doctors reserve for greeting their patients.

"Stop giggling, Ricardo!" I say, giggling myself.

No one speaks inside the room while we hear the sound of objects being placed on the night table—jars of medicines? *Tac, toc, tec,* the sounds vary. *Tac* and *toc* for the larger and medium sizes? *Tec* for the little jars? I think of the small night table and envision my mother removing the books to make space for the medicine jars.

"You think Papa will be all right, Marta?"

"I think so, yes! And you see the colonel is not such a bad man after all."

"I'm glad we went to speak to him."

We can't hear what my mother and the doctor are whispering while my father coughs in the background.

"I think he's going to allow us to have our meals at the base mess hall, the colonel."

"I hope so, Ricardo."

Not to go to the market ever again! Ricardo and I take turns "using our imagination" at the market, as Mama calls it. Begging is, in fact, what we have been doing.

Each time it is my turn to go, I take clothes to the campesina in exchange for a few fruits and vegetables that she throws in my basket reluctantly. I have taken a blouse, ribbons, one scarf, two pairs of panties, and even two shirts of my father's.

"That red dress, señorita, the one that don't have no buttons but little bows, the—" she told me last Saturday.

"Yes, I know!" I interrupted, but everyone around was still, listening.

"And I bring you fresh eggs next time."

Don Nicanor has continued to let us have the aspirins, alcohol, and soup bones. Sometimes he adds chicken feet and necks.

My mother sent her pearl brooch the other day. I had to force Don Nicanor to accept it "until we get the money from the city," I lied.

To add to my humiliation, Polo, to help, has developed his own beggar's act. While Don Nicanor disappears into the back of the store to get the soup bones, Polo heaves deep sighs and shakes his head mournfully, inviting everyone around to commiserate. "They have no pesos," he mutters to whoever is nearby. Word by word, he goes on reciting our calamities, "hungry," "boils," "sick." Polo is like the second half of those professional teams of beggars I have often seen on the street corners in our city.

"Stop it, Polo!" I say with clenched teeth, wishing I could give him a kick.

"¡Gracias, Don Nicanor, gracias!" he shouts, grabbing the package from Don Nicanor, who looks from me to him, somewhat mystified by the soldier's drama.

"Is there anything else, señorita?" Don Nicanor invariably asks.

Ricardo takes advantage of the question and frequently brings rice, beans, and always some corn for Perico.

"Whoever heard of a chicken as a pet," I said today before the doctor came. "Chickens are to be eaten." And that was what made Ricardo cry.

"Aspirins and alcohol," Mama is saying as she steps out, the doctor behind her. "I don't know how the villagers manage when they're sick."

"You may keep the thermometer, señora. Don't keep bothering him; I mean once a day is enough to take his temperature."

"He's very ill, isn't he, doctor?"

Doctor Martínez doesn't answer. It occurs to me that he's thinking she's a stupid woman to ask such a question.

My mother leads him into the living room while he fumbles for something in his valise. Ricardo and I also go in. The three of us look at the doctor, demanding that he answer her question.

"His heart is strong, but he needs . . . It's urgent to have Señor Maldonado in the hospital. That's my advice. Unfortunately, it doesn't depend on me. I'll give my report to Colonel Ferreira and he—they will decide."

"They?"

"Surely you understand, Señora Maldonado. Colonel Ferreira and those who give instructions concerning your husband."

"You may tell the colonel that any of your good army hospitals will do. I mean it doesn't have to be in our city, anywhere they decide."

The doctor is giving my mother a tiny jar he has just taken from the valise. "Six drops in half a glass of water every three hours, day and night."

"Six drops in half a glass of water every three hours, day and night," Mama repeats.

"This is a sample. I'll send you more. The drops will soothe his lungs and will allow him to sleep. Does he cough like this all the time?"

"All the time!" Mama, Ricardo, and I answer in unison.

"Difficult . . . yes, very difficult." He walks over to my brother. Pulling down Ricardo's eyelids, he looks at them for a moment. He presses his neck and behind his ears. "What are those?"

"Those are—they were boils," Mama answers with reticence, as though she has suddenly forgotten that he is the doctor, with whom she doesn't need to pretend. "He's all right now. He's been able to go to the market these past weeks."

The doctor comes over to me. He asks my age and goes through the same routine, touching my throat, pressing behind my ears.

"You're aware, I'm sure, that neither you nor your brother, any of you, should use your father's dishes."

"As you can see, doctor, my husband must be hospitalized."

He nods. His hooded eyes resemble my father's, but the disillusionment in the doctor's seems to have inhabited those eyes for years. His lips glisten with saliva; they are thick and dark like liver, but there is a pleasantness about the man.

Once more he's searching for something in his case. This time he brings out a roll of mints and a small cellophane package of half-smashed crackers. He moves his hand back and forth undecidedly, then offers them to Ricardo.

My brother takes the mints and the crackers, his eyes darting toward my mother. *"Gracias."*

"I am a glutton, always nibbling." He smiles and begins

157

moving toward the door to leave. "I'll send the drops to Señor Maldonado and vitamins for the three of you. I'll see that you get them as soon as possible. Unfortunately, I don't have . . . I wasn't prepared for your husband."

"And the hospital, doctor. Please try your best!"

"Yes, yes!" he says, but he opens his arms in a gesture of futility. At the door he turns. "I almost forgot!" He takes a paper out of his hip pocket. "Colonel Ferreira asked me to have you sign this, señora," he says, unfolding the paper.

"What is it?"

"It's a certificate stating that he, Colonel Ferreira, sent medical assistance to Señor Maldonado."

"Medical assistance?" Mama and I burst out.

"I am here and I am a doctor; that's what the colonel means."

He places the paper against the valise for Mama to sign. "Please, señora, here is my pen."

"I don't understand. I thought that sending you here, doctor, was the colonel's personal decision. Why does he want my signature?"

"You must understand, señora, that I'm simply conveying his message." He thrusts the valise forward, still offering the pen, which my mother does not take.

"Your signature may prompt Colonel Ferreira to action. Your husband is—he needs to be hospitalized!"

My mother takes the pen immediately. " 'I, Margarita de Maldonado,' " she reads aloud, " 'certify that Colonel Augusto Ferreira has provided medical assistance to my husband, Miguel Maldonado.' " She shakes her head for a moment, then signs. "I'm signing a lie!"

Doctor Martínez folds the paper and puts it back into his pocket. "You have no access to the news of the events that are taking place in the country, do you, señora? Well . . ." he says, moving away. At the door he pauses. "Powers

158

shift. . . . Let me say simply that Colonel Ferreira—we all
have our fears!" He takes long strides, leaving now, calling,
"¡Buenas tardes!"

My mother clutches the bottle of drops against her
bosom.

⌑ 21

"It's not raining! This morning I saw a white-crowned sparrow hopping about on the wall!" Mama calls. "And the yard is almost dry!"

Where does my mother find her energy? I wonder. All day long, every day, she moves from the bedroom to the kitchen, to the backyard and to my father again. Ricardo's chicken follows her everywhere. Even with closed eyes I can see my mother and Perico, the four skinny legs in short, jittery steps, Mama's chignon like a crest. I see two birds unequal only in size.

Doctor Martínez sent several tiny bottles of drops, all samples, and enough aspirins to last for weeks, but no word about hospitalization. In the package that the soldier brought, there were also vitamins for us and a tin of English crackers. Mama gave us one each day, and the last ones she broke in pieces as the priest does in church when there are more communicants than hosts.

The fight between Mama and Ricardo has started. It takes place every day at siesta, after she gives my father his drops and closes his bedroom door tightly.

"If nothing happens soon, I promise, Mama. Let's please wait another week."

160

"Listen, Ricardo. Today is Saturday and it was Marta's turn to go to the market, but the soldier didn't come. They sent no one, and now—"

"Polo is probably on duty at the mountain barracks, but he'll come next week, Mama—"

"And in the meantime . . . Listen, Ricardo, I'm getting tired of this. I've waited enough, hoping that you would be sensible."

"Marta, you heard what the doctor said, remember? He said that there is news, but because we don't read the papers—"

"He said something about newspapers, yes, but that doesn't mean anything," I say.

"You two! Papa would have understood what the doctor said, but you two, you!" He picks up his chicken and disappears into his room, closing the door.

"Let's wait, Mama, maybe something— Let's wait. Perico, he's one of us!"

"Don't be ridiculous, Marta!"

She shuffles back and forth for a while, then moves to Ricardo's room.

"Open the door!" she orders.

He runs out of the room, clutching Perico under one arm, holding the iron bar with the cutting edge in the other hand. With his long hair, my brother reminds me of a picture in one of the convent's halls: a shepherd boy holding a lamb in one arm, carrying his staff in the other hand.

Mama goes after him, and both rush to the entrance hall. She comes back after a moment.

Ricardo is outside, where the guard allows him to sit by the edge of the hill. Other afternoons he escapes to the backyard, down the embankment, out of Mama's reach. He returns after siesta, when the door of my father's room is open.

"You could help put some sense into your brother, you know!"

"I think Polo will come later, Mama. Maybe he's there. I thought I heard his voice talking to the guard a moment ago."

"Stop it, Marta! You're always imagining things, like the medicines that were supposed to be on the night table the day the doctor came. You're not a child; you're a woman, Marta, but what help do I get from you? All day on that chair dozing on and off, having fantasies. Go to your room, sleep, isn't that what you want to do all day long?"

"Beware, girls," Sister Tekla is saying. "Bad thoughts can sneak into your heads. Do you understand what I am saying?"

"Yes, Sister Tekla. I have an example. If it happens today, Mama, Ricardo, and I will go free tomorrow."

"If what happens today? Speak up clearly, Marta Maldonado!" The nun's face changes, and it's Mother Andrea who is shaking her finger at me.

I also see Uncle Alberto and my cousin Lucía.

"Martica, you have lost so much weight, and Ricardo, he looks comical with his long hair. Was it awful, Marta?"

"Not really. You see, we wrote compositions and read them to each other, and Perico, you should see the tricks Ricardo has trained his chicken to do! It kept Papa laughing until the end."

"Your example, Marta. Try again!" Sister Tekla's gray, watery eyes are looking at me.

"If my father . . ."

"Yes? If your father, go on!"

"If my father dies today, Mama, Ricardo, and I will go free!"

I wake up hearing a chuckle and low voices coming from the front door of the house. I must get up and find out, I urge myself, but I am too lazy to move.

Whispers and contained laughter continue.

I sit up and walk out.

Ricardo is in the corridor, facing the entrance hall. He is chewing.

"What are you eating, Ricardo?"

He wipes his mouth quickly.

"Pedro is here, Marta; he just came." He talks through his full mouth.

"What are you eating?" I push Ricardo. "Answer me!"

The soldier who guards the front door rushes out. I now see Pedro standing in the entrance hall, looking down as the chicken pecks at a pile of corn on the floor.

"What are you doing here?" I ask Pedro, but I am looking at the crumbs on Ricardo's mouth.

"I gave your brother a piece of bread and lumps of brown sugar," Pedro answers, searching his pockets. "I have a small piece," he says, bringing out a lump of brown sugar.

I grab it and put it in my mouth.

Pedro smiles, looking away, embarrassed.

"Have you been coming here every day, bringing food to my brother?"

"*Sí, señorita,* every day!" Pedro says proudly. "And corn to the chicken. Mostly we meet in the backyard." The soldier thrusts his chin forward, pointing at Ricardo. "He waits for me here or in the back if Señora Margarita isn't there, washing clothes."

Ricardo has been eating what Pedro brings him every day. He has shared nothing with me, I am saying to myself. My brother has thought only of himself and his chicken while Papa, Mama, and I are having one meager meal per day.

"Get out!" I shout, as if the bitterness building within me is against Pedro. "Out!"

Ricardo grabs his chicken and runs to his room.

I pick up the bar from the floor and march toward Ricardo's room.

"Open the door!" I bang the bar on the door, careless of the noise I am making. "Open up!"

I can hear the chicken's excited cackling.

"Wait!" Ricardo calls, but I force myself inside.

The chicken in his arm, Ricardo ducks to escape.

I shove the chicken out of his arm with the iron bar, then push the door closed. Ricardo slaps my face and tries to recover Perico.

The frightened chicken is flapping around the room, over our heads, expelling droppings. Finally he perches himself on the sill of the square window.

"Here, Perico, here!" Ricardo pats his arm, calling, "Here, jump, Perico!"

Head hidden between his wings, the bird has made himself into a ball and doesn't move.

"Perico, here!" Ricardo calls in vain.

After a moment he turns and attempts to take the bar away from me. We dance around each other, gasping, struggling with the bar.

"It's mine; give it to me!" Ricardo says, panting.

I see his fist coming but quickly I move backward. Holding the bar horizontally, I push it toward Ricardo, sending him across the room, against the wall.

"You hurt me!" he says, touching the back of his head, examining his fingers for blood. "You hurt me! Papa is listening!"

"Let him listen. Let him hear that you've been feeding yourself like a pig while Mama and Papa and I are hungry," I whisper harshly. "And I thought you were generous!"

164

"Shut up, Marta! Stop it, please!"

A voice inside me repeats, "Stop it!" Instead, I raise the bar and thrust it against the windowsill. I feel the bar's cutting edge piercing Perico's body.

With open wings the bird leaps and scratches at the window glass, then drops to the floor. He lies there, still; then, lifting himself, Perico moves sideways in short, jerky steps as if performing one final trick. Falling at last, the bird moves his wings weakly and goes on shuddering.

Ricardo looks from his chicken to me, bewilderment on his face.

The bar still in my hands, I keep hearing, "I killed Perico! I killed Perico!" My screams continue uncontrollably.

My mother is standing at the door of the room, her wet hair falling down over her shoulders.

"Are you going out of your mind, Marta? I could hear your screams in the backyard while I was bathing. What happened?"

She needs no answer.

On the floor, in a puddle of blood, lies Perico. Ricardo sits nearby, eyes closed, his face streaming with tears.

"Margarita, what's going on?"

"It's Marta and Ricardo. They're having an argument. Don't worry. I'll be with you shortly, Miguel."

She picks up the blood-dripping chicken and dashes to the kitchen.

From the door I watch my mother. Indifferent to Ricardo's and my grief, she is all energy as she moves about the kitchen, her robe unbuttoned, her naked body half-exposed.

Ricardo's blank face and stubborn silence kept me glancing at him covertly, while he, like I, devoured his pet.

After each bone was picked clean, we boiled them for broth.

Ricardo is in the hammock at all hours.

"It's not healthy. . . . Please!" Mama begins but lacks energy to impose her will.

From my chair by the door of my room, I see his foot as he lies in the hammock—the big toe sticking out of the dingy canvas shoe. My brother's toe seems to have an eloquence of its own. "I'll never forgive you, Marta," it says. "There's nothing now to distract my mind from reality!"

It's not only my father, I say to myself. I have also lost my brother, my friend.

"You should be pleased, Ricardo," Mama repeats. "Your chicken was a savior. Grow up!"

Pedro has continued to come at siesta hour, his pockets bulging with two or three eggs, tomatoes, "an orange for Don Miguel," and always the lumps of brown sugar. Pedrito is saving us from total starvation.

"I can bring only what fits in my pockets!" he often says gruffly. Is he impatient with himself because he cannot give us more, or is he blaming us for the risk he takes in coming here?

But something is changing at the base. The idleness of the soldiers, whom we hear playing *pompo* all day, is the only tangible difference. It's in the air, mostly, an uncertainty, a restlessness, as if the colonel and his men, like us, are also waiting, wondering about their fate. Even the laughter and drunken singing of Saturday nights seem less boisterous.

Last night we were awakened by the shouts of a man yelling "No, no!" There was shuffling of feet while the man continued screaming, calling his mother, *"¡Mi madre, mi madre!"* Then there was a shot, followed by that stillness that is more frightening than the noise of the bullets. In this place I've learned that silence can roar like thunder.

There are moments when I think I can walk down the hill

and wait for a truck or the bus that travels to the city, but all I want to do is to sleep and to eat.

The thought of Enrique Sarmiento, the twenty-two-year-old student who was taken prisoner after a speech against the dictator, comes to my mind. Enrique became a national hero. He spoke to himself in his cell constantly. The other prisoners would hear him arguing, laughing, calling his girlfriend, "Isabel, I brought you a carnation for your hair," and "Where shall we go tonight?"

"He is loco," the prison guards would say. At night Enrique sang and recited Federico García Lorca and Pablo Neruda. Even on his way to the prison yard to be executed, Enrique maintained the illusion that he was surrounded by his dear ones, speaking to them. "I will remain a human being until the end," he wrote with a nail on the wall of his cell.

I feel a surge of energy. I spring to my feet and approach the hammock. Ricardo's eyes are closed, and there's soot on his cheek; his mouth is half-open. My little brother! Will he ever be free? At the university will he feel the need to emulate his father and prove to himself and to others that he is the son of Miguel Maldonado? I extend my hand to touch his tousled hair, but I stop in midair. Without touching his face I trace the shape of his nose and his chin.

I will walk out of the house and go down to Don Nicanor's store to pawn my two rings and my earrings. I will bring bread, meat, cheese. I will come loaded with everything that fits in my arms. I will, I will, I will, I keep repeating to myself, as the temptation to return to my chair seizes me.

"Ricardo, I'm going down to the village to bring food. Ricardo!" He stirs and looks up at me, frowning, puzzled by my hand trembling in the air above his face.

"Food," he mutters and closes his eyes again.

The guard is seated on the floor, leaning against the door frame. He is stroking something with both hands. A chicken? A kitty?

It's not until I am standing behind him that I see. The soldier is stroking himself. I cover my face and run back into the house and to my chair. I've seen a man committing what Mother Andrea called the most degrading sin.

I tried, I say to myself. "But I did try!" I actually hear my own voice, as if I am arguing with someone. I feel relief that the incident with the guard forced me to run back into the house, saving me from pleading with Don Nicanor and from the exertion of climbing uphill with the load of food.

But I shall do something, I go on arguing with myself. I will be alert to Pedro's arrival at noon. I will find out if, indeed, there's a change taking place, a reason for hope. And just as I am formulating my resolution, I slip into my room to lie on my cot. I succumb to my animal state.

"Señora Margarita, Ricardo," Pedro calls, coming into the house.

"I'll be with you in a minute, Pedrito!" Mama half opens my father's bedroom door.

"I'll take care of it, Mama; go back."

He wants to see Ricardo, he insists, and I see that Pedro has no intention of emptying his pockets for me.

"Why are you mad at me, Pedro?"

"Perico—your brother told me everything. It's like you killed a human!"

"I didn't mean to do it. Pedro, you come here every day. Aren't you afraid, isn't it dangerous?"

"They don't care about this house anymore. Colonel Ferreira and Captain Paredes, they have other things pestering them."

168

"What things, Pedro, please tell me."

"Teniente Velez and his men were shot, eight of them, shot!"

"Who killed them?"

"I don't know. They were at the mountain barracks. And the next week, Captain Paredes and the men who were on duty, they—there are no campesinos alive up there. 'Just shoot and don't ask questions!' That's what he said. 'Put the fear in all of them. Shoot, shoot!' The butcher.'' Pedro's lips quiver as they quivered that night when he gave us the news about his godfather, Honorio. "They killed the women, the children, the donkeys, even the dogs, everything that moved. The colonel, he's also mean, but not as mean as Captain Paredes. They quarrel, those two—always bickering, the colonel and the butcher." He looks at me intently for a moment. "You're not having it so hard. To be hungry, that's not so bad. No one comes here to rape you or to shoot you. You and your—you're lucky!"

I am shocked and saddened by the hostility I see in the soldier's eyes. Risking himself on Saturday nights, coming here every day at noon to bring us what he can snatch from the base bodega, has nothing to do with friendship. Pedro is dominated by the ghost of his *padrino*.

As if guessing my thoughts, he says, "My godfather gives me no peace if I don't watch over Don Miguel. Those nights when the wind comes from the side of the mountain where he was killed, I hear his voice, my *padrino,* telling me to watch over Don Miguel. I want to go back to my village, like the others, Samuel, Gerónimo, even Teniente Rosado was running away. . . . But they got him last night. Didn't you hear? He was screaming like a woman. Didn't you hear?"

"I heard, yes."

"Polo, he ran away too, but you see that was before

Teniente Velez and his men were killed. Now they keep an eye on everybody!"

"What do you hear about the General, Pedro?"

"The General—the big General?" he asks, as though the dictator is a stranger. Like all campesinos, Pedro's concern is only with his immediate surroundings. He shrugs his shoulders. Then, yanking at his jacket as if to tear it apart, he says, "This military rag is no good anymore!"

He pats his pockets, glances along the corridor, and gives me nothing.

"I'll call Ricardo."

"Wait." He takes two eggs, one peach, and an orange from one pocket, and from the other pocket, a yucca and two more eggs. He unbuttons his jacket, and, smiling for the first time, he pulls out a package he has been sandwiching between his back and the jacket. It's a wet, bloodstained paper bag with a piece of meat and lumps of brown sugar, all thrown together. Finally he bends and brings out a banana hidden at his ankle, inside the boot. "This is for your brother. Tell him I'll bring a loaf of bread tomorrow."

"Maybe you can do me a favor, Pedro. Could you go to Don Nicanor and take this in exchange?" I begin to slide off my ring. "What about you and me, Pedro, could we go to Don Nicanor's store? I want to—"

"You want to get shot; you don't listen!"

"But you said that they don't care about us anymore!"

"As long as you don't leave the grounds and don't mess with anything. I come here when they're all sleeping siesta; the rest of the time I stay put." Looking around him as if someone may hear, he whispers, "At dawn, it's the only time, at dawn. . . ." But he doesn't finish.

"At dawn?"

"The butcher, he's never around until midmorning. He's the one with the hawk's eye, Captain Paredes."

I feel tired, standing there, holding the few things he has brought us.

"I'm leaving. I must go!" Pedro says, with such intensity I realize he's talking about going to his village.

"The banana is for Ricardo," he repeats before going away.

⧉ 22

"A miracle, it's like a miracle!" Mama exclaims. "Marta, Ricardo, come and see!"

I have no curiosity for the wonder Mama is announcing. As usual, I wait for my brother to answer. I look up at the window. The sky is still dark, but the church bells have begun. No one comes to escort us to the market anymore—Saturdays are like any other day.

"Marta, come, look!" Ricardo says.

I walk out of my room, getting into my robe.

My mother and Ricardo are trying to lift a huge basket onto the table. The basket is bursting with fruits, greens, eggs, bread, and cheese wrapped in banana leaves. The kitchen table is already covered with things Mama and Ricardo have taken out.

"Enough food to feed an army," Mama says, her eyes shining.

"Who brought it, Mama? It's the biggest basket I've ever seen; who brought it?" I rub my eyes.

She heard steps in the kitchen very early. She thought it was Ricardo looking for something to eat. "And I said to myself, I'll give him a cup of boiling water with a lump of brown sugar. The basket was right there. I thought I was hallucinating!"

"You think that Don Nicanor perhaps . . ." Ricardo and I ask.

"I think some of these things were bought at dawn at the market and others were probably taken from the base food storage. I suspect Pedrito, who else?" She smiles.

Ricardo and I are each eating a banana, while touching and smelling every item, opening the bags of rice and beans with wonder, as if they are Christmas gifts.

"Please, please!" Mama says, hands to her face. Then, slapping Ricardo's hand, which is pinching the cheese, she says, "Take an orange, a piece of bread, here. . . . Here, but leave me alone for a moment, please!" She wants to assess the contents of the basket, the number of days it should last. "We can't afford to think only of today. It must last! Such a big basket!"

But her hands, which were moving hastily, are now still, resting on the basket. Her face darkens as if it's wrong for us to be excited. She's thinking of my father, of course. In a moment she will go to the bedroom to report "the miracle." She tells him all the everyday occurrences. Yesterday I heard, "Miguel, something is changing at the base. Pedro told Ricardo that Colonel Ferreira has gone to the city, taking his family with him, and that there are rumors he's not coming back. That the colonel was lying when he said he was going to the city to discuss some matters with his superiors." She waited for Papa to answer. "Ah, Miguel, if you would speak and tell us something. You always know!"

"Wait! Listen!" Ricardo says now. There are footsteps in front and in back of the house.

"Quickly!" Mama mutters, and we begin putting things back into the basket. Then we slide out from under it the bedspread that is used as a tablecloth. Mama throws the bedspread over the basket.

We hear shots. One bullet crosses the sky over the yard.

Two soldiers charge into the house from the front, their rifles pointed at us.

I scream, and Mama and I grab at each other.

"Where is he?" a man shouts in the entrance hall. It's Captain Paredes; he has a pistol in his hand.

Simultaneously, an officer and four soldiers stamp from the backyard into the kitchen. The soldiers are carrying rifles; the officer, a pistol. Some walk into the linen room; the others, into Ricardo's and my rooms.

"*Dios mío, Dios mío,*" Mama says over and over.

"They are coming after my father," I hear my voice.

"You're hiding him. Where is he?" Captain Paredes pushes the door of my father's room.

My mother detaches herself from me to confront the captain. "Don't disturb my husband! He's a sick man. Don't go in, please!"

With his free hand, Captain Paredes pushes my mother, his open hand against her face.

Mama stumbles backward, losing her balance, falling down slowly until she sits against the corridor wall.

Ricardo and I dash to her. "Don't say anything, Mama, please!" we plead as we help her to her feet.

The house is filled with military men. They are in the kitchen, the yard, going in and out of the rooms.

"Who's lying there?" Captain Paredes yells inside my father's room.

Mama struggles to free herself from Ricardo's and my grip. "Please, Mama, please!" But she manages to shove us away and hurries inside.

She has no sense; she's crazy, my mother. She will get us all killed. Maybe that's what she wants, to finish with everything once and for all. But I want to live!

Her courage or her senselessness has no limits. "Can't

you see that there is a sick man in here?'' she's shouting.

"He's hiding somewhere else!'' the officer calls. Two soldiers follow him, and the three leave through the back.

Sheets, blankets, underwear, and Ricardo's and my cots have been thrown in the corridor and the yard.

The captain steps out into the corridor.

Another officer appears and struts across the yard, waving his pistol, then turns around, as if he's leaving. He stands in the center of the yard, near the hammock, and shoots in the air. He addresses me. "Under martial law, anyone who hides deserters is punished with the death penalty; you know that, don't you?'' I recognize the man. It's the one who speaks with closed lips like a ventriloquist and who took Honorio's bouquet of dry herbs. "There are two soldier fugitives; one of them comes here at noon every day.''

"Yes, Teniente Rojas,'' answers a soldier standing nearby. "He comes bringing them things to eat.''

"Pedro!'' I say foolishly.

"Let's go!'' says Captain Paredes, stamping out of Ricardo's room. "Anyone who attempts to leave will be shot!'' But I have the feeling that the captain is saying this for the benefit of the soldiers who are still in the house. "We'll put an end to this, damn it!''

Mama is standing by the door to my father's room.

"¡Nadie, mi Capitán!'' reports a soldier, walking out of my room. "We looked everywhere.''

"Out!'' Captain Paredes waves his pistol at the men. "What the hell are you waiting for? Move! Find the two cowards. Shoot them on sight!''

Just as he's about to disappear through the entrance hall, he whirls around and looks at my mother. "We cannot permit traitors to go free. You understand!'' he says, with a hint of apology.

175

His complexion is a bilious green; his pregnantlike belly protrudes even more than the first time we saw him. He has a second pistol on his hip.

Mama, Ricardo, and I stand there, saying nothing. We look at the mess around us. The tablecloth has been pulled away from the basket. A smashed egg is on the floor, and some oranges have rolled off, but nothing has been taken away. Pages of *Don Quixote,* which was in my room, are fluttering everywhere. I begin to pick them up.

"Marta, give something to Ricardo and—" Mama is pale, exhausted, as if she's about to faint. "You both eat. Take care; it must last, remember." She's trembling, and her voice is barely audible. Her eyes look away from Ricardo, who is now lying facedown on the hammock, whimpering, mumbling, "Pedrito!"

"I'll take care of everything; you rest, Mama."

But the guard who stands by the door is running into the house. "They found them! They were nearby in the yard of Señor and Señora Lozada. They found them!"

Ricardo runs to the front door.

"You don't want to see. . . . Come, Ricardo, let's eat something!" I go after him.

We hear several shots, and for a moment there is silence. Then someone shouts, "They killed them!"

The house where they found Pedro and his friend, the guard explains, is across from the fort's entrance.

The plaza is almost empty. Campesinos and villagers have left everything to come and watch. More are coming, crossing the main road. They are running and screaming, some falling. Children wail; dogs bark. A few boys are climbing the wall around the fort. Several men have already installed themselves on the roof of a bus parked on the road across from us.

"They are bringing them!" a voice yells. "They are coming!" Everyone shouts, "They are coming!"

I wonder why they bring the bodies around instead of taking them into the fort through the back entrance, across from the house where they found them. Captain Paredes, no doubt, wants everyone to see. I remember what Pedro told me about the man's orders, "Put fear into them!"

Captain Paredes is now walking through the gate. Behind him soldiers drag the bodies by their feet, as the campesinos drag the sacks of potatoes and yuccas at the market.

I put my arms around my brother, trying to cover his face. His mouth open, he's making strange noises, pulling away, as if in need of air. His head jerks like that of a wild pony.

"Let's go in, Ricardo." I turn to the guard. "Please help me."

"Yes, señorita." He takes Ricardo's arm. "Don't cry, hombre! Don't cry!" But, hearing the screams of a woman, the guard drops my brother's arm and quickly turns back to the door to watch.

"Look! They have Señor and Señora Lozada!" the guard announces.

I lead Ricardo inside.

The loud crying of the woman increases. Her screams are piercing.

"What's happening, Marta? Why is that poor woman screaming?" Mama comes out of the bedroom.

"They found Pedrito and the other soldier in their yard, the woman's. But what's the matter with you, Mama?"

"I just can't stop this trembling; it will pass," she says, shaking all over, glancing at Ricardo. "Come, dear, let's have something to eat." She puts her arm around his shoulder.

"*Mi comandante,* we are innocent!" a man now screams.

Mama's hands flutter over the kitchen table. "I'll make some coffee," she says, grabbing her hands as if to steady them. "There is a bag of coffee somewhere; I saw it." She takes one of the breads.

Ricardo is back in the hammock, which rocks under his sobs.

"Slice the cheese, Marta," my mother says.

"We didn't hide anybody! We didn't know the soldiers were hiding in our house! Oh, God!" We hear the voices now as if they are in our own yard.

"There!"

"The coffee?"

"Right there!"

"The jelly? What is it, Mama?"

"The couple, Marta, the couple! They are right there in the base yard!" she shouts, dropping the bread, clutching me. "Let's go into your father's room; let's leave all this for a moment. Come!"

Ricardo is now in front of the kitchen table, snatching a piece of bread. I have a chunk of cheese in my mouth.

We hear grunting and scuffling.

"The children! Oh, God! Felipe, Roberticooo!" the man and woman call in unison.

We clasp each other, Mama's and my trembling fusing as we drag ourselves along the corridor toward the bedroom.

"Shoot!" a voice orders.

Two shots break the air.

We halt. "No!" An acute scream perforates my ears. It takes me a moment to realize it's my mother's, and I cover her mouth.

She gasps, trying to push me away, her eyes enlarged with terror.

"Shhh, shhh!"

She nods. Immediately I pull away from her and, with Ricardo, we walk to the kitchen, slowly first, then rushing. To eat!

With a full stomach the mind becomes clear; all faculties sharpen. Human pain replaces obsession with survival. Guilt is here to stay. It's our fault about Pedro, just as it was about his godfather, Honorio. It's our fault that they killed the Lozadas.

In my mind I see the couple at all hours. Some Saturdays we would find ourselves with the Lozadas, walking along the little street leading to the plaza—the man and the woman with their two sons, one of them Ricardo's age, the older retarded. Their hair wet and shining, their clothes neat and starched, the four would stride to the market with an air of anticipation. The couple would talk between themselves, in subdued voices, pretending not to notice us. The retarded boy made guttural noises, pointing at Ricardo and me, excited by our presence.

I think of the last time I saw Pedro. "He gives me no peace, my godfather. Those nights when the wind comes from the side of the mountain where he was killed, I hear his voice, my *padrino,* telling me to watch over Don Miguel." With the generous gift of the basket, Pedro thought he was at last free of the ghost of Honorio. "No one comes here to rape you or to shoot you. You don't have it so bad. You're lucky!" I recall the words of our loyal friend.

▣ 23

Since they executed Pedro and the Lozada couple, three weeks ago, we know nothing of the world outside this house. We move like the blind, guided by the surrounding sounds, or rather by their absence. But this is a new silence—a silence charged with promise, like the pause in a musical composition preceding the next movement. "Listen. . . . Wait. . . . Be alert," the air seems to murmur. One senses that the village, the country, the whole world is expectant.

Ricardo looks out the window for the first time this morning.

"The guard is not by the door, Marta."

Have we become so insignificant that they do not need to keep us under their custody? I wonder.

"And there are no jeeps or trucks parked in front of the building. There's garbage everywhere."

"They are probably at the mountain barracks," I say. "You think perhaps we can go out, Ricardo, and learn what's going on?"

"Maybe, yes," he says but walks to lie down in the hammock. "I'll go out after Mama gives us today's meal."

Mama hides the few things that are left from Pedrito's basket. Hiding food and distributing our frugal daily portions take up all her strength.

I resent her apathy. She spends most of her time now on the chair near my father's cot. There are moments one could easily believe they have died together inside the room. Two or three times a day, Ricardo or I open the door to check on them and, of course, we hear the whistle of Papa's respiration, which replaces his cough lately. We keep looking until our eyes get accustomed to the darkness. Then we see our mother's back, her hunched, thin shoulders moving as she breathes.

"Marta, my rings, your earrings," she said yesterday, after she gave us our meal. "We need food. Do something!" Overcome by lethargy, she closed her eyes and walked away.

"What can I do? You don't care anymore, Mama!"

She has abandoned us to our own resources. It's up to us now to survive.

My brother searches for food in drawers and between the linens, inside the empty suitcases and in every place he suspects Mama may have hidden something. He moves about, sniffing like a rat. The other day there was a stench. He followed it until he found a piece of rotten cheese Mama had forgotten, concealed in a corner behind a pot.

I have lost my appetite and feel nauseous most of the time, but within me something throbs: my determination to stay alive.

In spite of the cold and the wind, it feels good to be out. I must not look toward the base, I tell myself, as I start downhill. Someone will espy me in a moment. I will hear a shout—"*¡Alto!*"—then the bullet coming toward me. And yet I am not afraid. I have an odd conviction that no one is going to see me, that I am safe.

To fight my temptation to turn toward the base, I concentrate on what's ahead of me. I notice the small trees down at the bottom of the hill. They have not reached full growth—the smooth trunks sway in the wind, trembling like tender calves. I look at the mountains ahead. One is shaped like a hunchback with a hat; another resembles a distant castle half covered by fog; and to my right, against a patch of clearing sky, the mountain has the appearance of a lion watching over the pueblo.

At last I am out of the fort. There's no one around. Such is the stillness that I wonder if the base and the pueblo have been evacuated.

As I am about to cross the main road, I see someone approaching. It's an old campesino with a stick in one hand. A few steps ahead is his burro with a load of dry branches on its back.

"Buenas tardes." He lifts his hat repeatedly but scowls, as if inconvenienced by my presence. "Not a good day to be out!" he says. He is no doubt referring to the weather, which is no different from any other day, even at this time of the year they call summer.

"Have you seen any buses going to the city?" I ask.

"Today?" He stops and gives me his profile. "No one wants to get burned in the big blaze. They say a war is going on in the capital and that it's coming this way, they say!" He looks up at the sky, as if he's talking about an approaching storm.

"Adios, señorita." He wants to be under his own roof; he goes on mumbling.

I don't catch his last words. He's trotting behind his burro and holding on to his hat, accelerating.

I stop by the edge of the main road, wondering what to make of the campesino's talk. Don Nicanor will give me news. If the store is closed, I will find him in his house. I cross the road.

I hear faraway voices. The air pulsates with the sound of laughter and singing. Do I imagine it?

There's a loud noise, like a stampede reverberating on the ground under my feet. I stop, frightened, remembering the campesino's words about the war coming this way. I walk over to one of the houses on the little street that leads to the plaza and knock on the window. No one answers. I move to the next house and pound on the door and keep pounding with my fists. "Please, please!"

Finally I turn back to cross the road again and return to the fort. I now hear a roar growing, reaching a crescendo. Should I hide? But I see no one at the fort, and quickly I start uphill. I feel light-headed and dizzy as I keep plodding.

And then clearly I hear the horses' hooves beating against the pavement of the main road, resounding like a thousand castanets. I stop midway up the hill. Horsemen are waving their hats, yelling *"¡Al fin!"* and that scream, "At last!" seems to erupt from every corner of the earth.

"¡Viva la libertad!"

"¡Vivaaaa!"

Overcome by fatigue and exhilaration, I sit by the door of the house, but only for an instant. The pounding of my heart repeats at last, at last, at last!

"Ricardo!"

He is still in the hammock.

"Have you heard, Ricardo, the shouts and *vivas*?"

His face comes to life as he sits up and listens.

"Come and see the cavalcade. I think they're landowners. They're coming from the direction of the city. Come!"

The plaza is slowly filling with people. It's as if the villagers were waiting behind their doors for a signal. They run in every direction, gesturing, bumping into one another like the ants in my room.

Ricardo points toward the base. The side door to the veranda is banging in the wind. A sickly dog is sniffing the ground; an old military boot lies among the debris outside the building.

"They are all gone, Marta, gone!" Ricardo repeats, pulling at my cardigan.

Someone has climbed the church tower, and the bells are ringing. The birds that nest in the belfry are flying over the plaza.

We rush out of the room, calling, "Mama, Papa, it's all over, all over!" Mama motions with her hand for us not to scream, but we can't stop describing the cavalcade and the shouts. ". . . and there's no one at the base; that's why we didn't hear any noises coming from there. They're all gone!"

She looks at us for a long time. "Are you sure?"

"Listen to the cheers!"

"And to the bells!"

"I hear them, but still . . . Are you sure?" She smooths her hair as if we are announcing that some visitor is outside. She gets up from her chair and bends over Papa. "Miguel, it's all over. Can you hear, Miguel, the church bells? Marta and Ricardo say that—"

There is no change in his face.

Excitement has made Ricardo and me forget that for the past days our father has been lying immobile, his eyes staring at the ceiling.

Her face close to his ear, she repeats, "It's all over; we'll go home and you'll be fine again, Miguel!" The three of us watch the unchanged countenance of my father.

Covering her face with both hands, Mama returns to the chair. She's crying.

I suddenly realize that for the first time since we have been in this house, I am seeing my mother cry. She has been angry, tender, unfair. She has been comical and valiant. Mama has displayed every emotion, but crying in front of us she has restrained. She's not sobbing. Hers is a quiet weeping. The tears fall gently, bathing her face, dropping down to her hands, now crossed on her lap. They keep pouring, as if from an everlasting source.

It occurs to me that crying is my mother's only act of kindness toward herself since we have been here.

Mama did not allow herself much comfort. After a moment she wiped her tears, changed into fresh clothes, and drank half a cup of weak, reheated coffee. "I am going down to the pueblo for help," she says now.

"You stay here, Mama; I'll go!" Ricardo offers. "I'll find a telephone."

She's about to disagree, then says, "I'll give you something to eat first."

She gives him soda crackers, a piece of guava sweet, and a cup of hot, diluted brown sugar. "Listen, Ricardo. Call Doctor Camacho; find him at home or at the hospital, but get ahold of him! Here are his telephone numbers. Explain, oh, dear, do you think you can—"

"I know what to say, Mama!"

Just as Ricardo has changed clothes and is about to leave, we hear a vehicle coming up the hill.

From the window we see a dilapidated black car. It's the mayor's Ford, the only nonmilitary car in the village, although most of the time the mayor drives a jeep or an official shiny sedan.

The Ford moves shakily up the hill path. The driver and two men in straw hats are in front. We can also see two heads in the backseat. The car puffs and gives up in midhill. The mayor gets out from the back. Behind him is a skinny little boy carrying a papaya as big as he is.

The mayor leans against the car and seems to be giving

instructions to the men in the front seat. He gestures, signaling the base.

A procession of campesinos is on the main road. Some are riding donkeys; some are on foot; all wave colorful handkerchiefs and move on their way to the city. A man is playing a tune that resembles the national anthem on his harmonica.

The Ford backs downhill to the path that leads directly to the base parking lot. The picture of the dictator that was glued to the rear window has been removed. The small national flags that were at either side of the picture are still there.

The mayor straightens his tie and buttons his coat. With the little boy at his heels, he's climbing toward us.

"What is that man coming here for? What nonsense now?" Mama says.

Shall we close the doors, ignore him? But Mama tells Ricardo to ask the man in.

"Congratulations!" the mayor calls, as if he's an old friend coming to share the good news with us.

"Señora Maldonado, señorita!" He bows, showing a bald spot emerging from a cobweb of seedy black hair. "I would like to offer my greetings to Don Miguel."

Mama stares at the man steadily, a sardonic smile on her lips. "My husband is resting!"

"I am here to reassure Don Miguel that you can count on my protection. These moments during the transition of power can become unexpectedly dangerous. I have lived through several. You see, señora, I have been the mayor of this pueblo for more years than I care to remember."

"I don't believe that we need your protection at this time. In any case, thank you," she says, moving backward to indicate that she considers his visit finished.

"I am sure, Señora Maldonado, that you wish to call your relatives, a friend? I have the only telephone in the village."

My mother's face softens. She retraces the steps she took backward. "Well, yes, as a matter of fact, my son here was about to leave in search of a telephone to call . . . my family!"

"But, my dear señora, *mi querida señora.* Today it's impossible to find a free line. The country is in chaos!" He opens his arms dramatically.

There is the noise of gears grinding.

"What's that?" Mama asks.

"It's . . . it's one of my trucks, señora. As I was saying a moment ago, I am a bit apprehensive of what the villagers in their excitement may do tonight. I fear looting." He raises his eyebrows.

"I see," Mama says absentmindedly. It's easy to guess that she is trying to find a way to convince the mayor that she must get in touch with Doctor Camacho today.

The little boy shifts the weighty papaya from one arm to the other.

"But, please, señora, let's sit down." The mayor sweeps his arm toward the living room, as if he's our host. "You first, señora."

My mother doesn't move and keeps wringing her hands slowly.

The mayor notices my eyes on the boy's tiny figure, which is bending backward under the huge papaya.

"I almost forgot. My wife Josefina sends this papaya to you. It's from our orchard. Here, Señora Maldonado, do me the honor." He takes the papaya from the boy and offers it to Mama, bowing ceremoniously.

"Thank you, but I expect we'll be leaving shortly, and the papaya shouldn't go to waste."

"Please, señora," he repeats and thrusts the fruit at Ricardo, whose eyes shift between Mama and me while he resists his impulse to grab it.

The man walks into the living room, carrying the papaya, searching for a place to unload it. Finally he sets it on one of the chairs and then puts his hat on top of it.

"Señor Alcalde, is there a way to catch a bus or rent a car? It's imperative that my son or I . . . we must reach the city today!"

"It's not only impossible but dangerous. You see, there are still small groups fighting in some sectors. I myself would not venture into the city at this point. Soon it'll be dark and your son, he is a child, and you . . . a woman! I'm telling you the facts. Please believe me, Señora Maldonado," he says softly, pronouncing each word slowly, as if he's dealing with a stubborn child.

My mother begins to rub her forehead.

"Since a week ago, when the news that the General was hiding in the Spanish Embassy began circulating, the city has been inaccessible. There are ugly rumors about vendettas— the kind of violent and uncivilized acts that usually take place at these moments. You understand, señora!" The mayor speaks as if he has been a victim of the military regime and one of the men who struggled to overthrow the dictator. I have often heard my father referring to politicians like the mayor; *"los reptiles,"* they are called, benevolent tyrants of small pueblos who never pronounce themselves against the ruling power and who go along with whatever happens to be the country's current political movement.

He turns to the little boy, who is leaning against the wall with his arms crossed, enjoying what's going on. "Go now, Paco!"

The child steps forward, lifts his hand to his brow, and in

a nasal voice recites, *"Buenas tardes, señores y señoritas. ¡Viva mi General!"*

"Shut up! Out!" yells the mayor, snapping his fingers.

Ricardo stifles a laugh.

"Slow . . . to the left . . . slow!" someone says at the base.

Ricardo and I approach the window. One of the mayor's men is giving instructions to the ones who are dragging a desk out through the front door. "Slow . . . careful!"

Outside the base there are tables, chairs, lamps. A big truck is parked in front.

"What's going on over there?" Ricardo asks.

"Where? Ah, yes . . ." Words fail the mayor at last. "As I was saying before, the city is inaccessible, señora."

My mother nods. She is concentrating on her own thoughts. "Excuse me, I must check on my husband." She walks away from the door.

The men are now moving glasses and bottles and making a racket.

The mayor scowls.

Ricardo and I are beginning to understand. Part of the mayor's purpose in coming here is to distract us while his men loot the deserted base.

"Ricardo!" Mama's voice comes into the room, and my brother rushes out.

"Your father, señorita, you should be very proud. Don Miguel was a powerful voice in the event the country is celebrating today!"

I glance away.

"He is sick, isn't he? He is a very sick man, your father, no?"

This time I look straight into his face without answering.

"I had your father very much in mind when you and my

nephew . . . But you young people, you just follow your little hearts!" With his index finger he taps his chest repeatedly. "Were you aware that in leaving this . . . your confinement, to meet my nephew, you were endangering your family?"

I do not bother to answer.

I can hear my mother's and Ricardo's hushed voices outside the room.

The mayor's nostrils quiver as he goes on looking at me, demanding an answer. My silence has wounded him.

"My nephew, you may like to know, now enjoys a very good position. He is the principal in Marañón's school." He makes an odd sound, and I realize he's chuckling as he adds, "He wouldn't recognize you now. You've changed a great deal, señorita!"

"I've made a decision, Señor Alcalde!" My mother bursts into the room. "You say you are here to help us. I believe you! Please provide us with transportation. You have trucks, jeeps, a car at your disposal. My son must be driven to the house of my brother in the city. Tonight! My husband's friends will be thankful. They won't forget that you helped us!"

The mayor springs to his feet. My mother's words have caught him off guard. A hand across his mouth, he gives the impression that he's considering alternatives, thinking deeply. After a moment he says, "I understand your urgency, señora, but I cannot send anyone to the city. I cannot endanger your son's life or the lives of my men. But I will get your family or whoever you wish to contact on my telephone. I'll try all night if necessary. You can count on me!" He's fumbling in his pockets, a pencil already in his hand.

"Here are the numbers," Ricardo says, giving him a piece of paper. "My uncle's house and—"

"The first person you must contact is Doctor Camacho!" my mother interrupts. "On that paper are both his home and hospital numbers. And tell him, please, where we are and to send an ambulance as soon as possible!"

The mayor, who has been studying the telephone numbers, gives a start. "An ambulance? Ah, señora, is Don Miguel that sick? I had no idea!" Such is the consternation on his face that it looks as if he's actually going to burst into tears. Picking up his hat, he marches out. At the door he twirls around. Holding his hat against his chest, the mayor bows with solemnity. "Señora Maldonado, I will take care of this. Trust me!" He shakes the paper with the telephone numbers. "I will get Don Miguel's doctor!"

The Ford is now waiting at the bottom of the hill. The truck is nearly full. Two men are stretching a tarpaulin to cover the furniture and the other items taken from the base. The other men talk and laugh while swigging from bottles.

⊡ 24

They came, as my father had predicted, our relatives and his friends.

At noon, while we were around his cot, we heard car doors slamming and a tumult of voices, some of which we recognized. Mama and Ricardo leaped to their feet and rushed out of the room. I stood by the door, hiding.

How many times had I dreamed of the moment they would come and my father would say, "See? We are going home at last!" Now that the moment had arrived, I did not want to see any of them.

"Margarita, is it you, my dear, my dear!" Uncle Alberto was exclaiming in the entrance hall. There were sniffles. "Ricardito, let me embrace you!"

Uncle Alberto and Aunt Lila were the first to come into the house. I saw them through the half-open doorway. Tall, well-dressed, they looked handsomer than I remembered. Their presence lit the corridor in spite of their solemn faces and dark clothes. I was startled by the contrast with my mother's cadaverous appearance, to which I had grown accustomed. Now, close to her older brother, my mother was an old woman. He and Aunt Lila held Mama by the arms, guiding her cautiously, as though she were disabled.

My cousin Lucía was behind them, one arm around Ricardo. With her clear pink complexion, her shiny hair falling to her shoulders, Lucía looked healthy and beautiful. She was wearing a bright red woolen dress and gold jewelry. "Marta, where is Marta?" Lucía asked.

More cars were arriving, and there was a constant slamming of doors. Uncle Alberto apparently had called everyone after the mayor contacted him. The house was small for the visitors, mostly men in dark suits, familiar faces I had seen many times around my father.

They walked into the house talking loudly but fell silent for a moment when they saw Mama, who was now in a chair by the door of the living room.

There was no end to the exclamations. "Where is Miguel? I left everything to drive here and congratulate him!" and "So this is the place—this horrible house. Ah, the courage and forbearance! Did someone bring a camera?"

"A camera!" several voices echoed.

My mother alone seemed composed, forcing smiles, speaking softly, raising a hand to indicate that no one was to go in to see my father until the doctor arrived. "Are you sure, Alberto, that Dr. Camacho and the ambulance—"

"They'll be here shortly, Margarita. Don't upset yourself!" Uncle Alberto reassured her. There had been a problem with the ambulances, he explained. "Several were destroyed and burned the day of the final confrontation to overthrow the dictator."

"Where is Marta?" Aunt Lila and Lucía inquired.

Mama explained that I was with my father but would be out in a moment.

Foolishly, I looked around the room, as if I could discover a secret exit or a place to hide. I dreaded having Lucía and the others see me. I myself had stopped looking at my face in the mirror.

The triviality of my concern, while my father was lying unconscious, added to my distress.

I walked over to his cot. His expression was unchanged, but there was a serenity in his countenance where the cheekbones stood out defiantly. His pallor threw a glow on the pillow.

"If I could make him understand that his struggle was not in vain!" Mama had repeated over and over.

"It's all we're asking, that Papa understand that his country and his family are all right!" I prayed. "That's all!" I heard myself muttering. And as I looked at the crucifix above him, I felt as if I were giving a friend the last chance to prove Himself.

"Marta." Ricardo pushed the door open. "Everyone is asking about you!"

I smoothed my hair and quickly stepped into the light of the corridor.

"¡Hola!" I called as casually as if I had seen them all a moment before.

"Marta? It can't—of course it's you, Martica." Aunt Lila came over with open arms. "Querida."

I heard sniffles and felt arms around me. "Martica." Had they loved me so much before? Wasn't it pity now? I must not cry, I told myself. I must not cry! I felt my face against tweed and the aroma of fine tobacco in my nostrils. A sob broke out of me. "There . . . there . . ." Uncle Alberto patted my head. "Here, Marta." My uncle offered me a handkerchief. I did not take it. Like the true daughter of my peasant father, I wiped my face with my hands.

"No one goes in!" Mama said sternly to a man who was following her as she stood up to go and check on my father.

Everyone was talking at the top of his voice. Only the words "Very ill" and "Poor thing" were uttered in whispers.

Uncle Alberto was thanking everybody for being there. "Margarita and I are most grateful!"

I noticed that the mayor and his stout wife—she wearing the catlike fur—were also there. Subdued and in a corner of the yard by the side of the kitchen, they kept their distance from the others, who ignored them.

Uncle Alberto alone addressed the mayor once to thank him for his telephone call. "It was most thoughtful of you. We knew they were here, but we were so . . . confused. You can understand our situation. It has been a long nightmare. But your call—it was very kind of you to let us know!"

"I only did my duty," the mayor answered. "I promised Señora Maldonado that I wouldn't sleep until I made the connections with the city."

"Was it awful, Marta?" Lucía asked.

The answers I had so often rehearsed did not come.

"It was terrible for us, Marta! You can't imagine how awful it got to be at the end. So many were killed, and there were bombs and burnings everywhere. We had to send the help to do the shopping. We didn't dare go out. Why, not even to the post office, you know. The only safe place was the country club. Mama and I and our friends spent most of our days there, and Papa would pick us up before the curfew."

"The ambulance!" someone announced. Aunt Lila approached the bedroom and called from the door, "Margarita, dear, the ambulance at last." The wailing of the siren was nearing.

"I'll never forget that horrible howling of the siren!" Lucía said, her pretty, long-nailed hands over her ears.

I couldn't help wondering how heavy my cousin's load of dark memories was.

In no time Doctor Camacho was inside the house, followed by two male hospital attendants carrying a stretcher and a nurse carrying medical equipment. Uncle Alberto rushed to guide them into the bedroom. Presently my uncle emerged with closed eyes, wagging his head. He stood still in front of the closed door, an actor in the center of the stage.

There was a moment of silence—all were trying to listen to the hushed voices inside the bedroom.

The entrance hall was filled with townspeople, attracted by the ambulance, a novelty in the pueblo. Outside the living room window were more faces with large, peering eyes.

My father's name was on everybody's lips. "Miguel was the first who alerted the country to the torture of political prisoners" and "We are indebted to Miguel!" and "A journalist obsessed by justice and truth, that's who he is, Miguel Maldonado." Someone called him a hero.

I recalled something my father had said one evening in our home in the city, after discovering that he was losing friends because of his editorials against the dictator. He said, "Many are calling me a traitor. You see, one is either a hero or a traitor. Nothing in between pleases my countrymen."

The hammock was swaying with the comings and goings of the visitors. Suddenly the ugly house was becoming dear. It was filled with my father's presence, the echo of his words. "They will come, my friends . . . and who knows, maybe Uncle Alberto will also be here to drive us to the city. Everyone will say his short speech. It will be a little ridiculous and tiresome . . . but we'll survive our small glory."

Risking nothing, they had come at last, indeed. They are here, I thought with bitterness, to partake in the momentary glory of "my brother-in-law," "my uncle," "my friend." They know how to play the national sport. How many of them, I wondered, like the mayor, are perennial members of the winning team?

My father was in a coma, yet I felt he was more alive than the ones moving about, patting each other's backs, repeating their empty phrases. I leaned against the hammock. How strange that, of all the emotions overwhelming me at that moment, I was not feeling my father's absence. His presence was powerful, and I knew at that instant that it would always be with me.

"Marta, could you help us, please?" a voice called behind my back. It was Alarcón, a journalist. His weekly magazine had also been closed by the government. Shortly afterward he had flown abroad with his family.

"Where are Miguel's papers, what he wrote here?"

"I think he tore them up. Maybe my mother . . . We packed this morning!" I pointed at a corner near the entrance hall and at the black case with the Remington.

"Margarita, no doubt, knows," a white-haired man with Alarcón said softly. "We must wait."

"We need Miguel's notes," Alarcón spoke again. "We're devoting an issue of my magazine to Miguel and García, to José and Murillo and Hernández, and all the others who—"

"Hernández?"

"He disappeared shortly after you left the city," the older man explained. "No one knows. . . . Rather we know only too well Juan Hernández's fate. He circulated an open letter asking about your father and your family. He received threats against his life but kept up a public protest on your behalf."

I covered my face.

"But we mustn't speak about this, not now. I am so sorry," he apologized.

"We want very much to have some of Miguel's writing," Alarcón said. "Your father was the main inspiration for this issue. It will be titled 'The Indispensable Men.'"

The door of the bedroom opened at last. The stretcher with my father, his eyes and forehead visible, came out.

Voices began calling Ricardo's and my name, offering us transportation to the city.

"Thank you," my mother answered, "but Marta and Ricardo will ride with me in the ambulance."

"Adios, señora, señorita, adios, niño!" the townspeople followed us downhill, calling.

"Good-bye. . . !"

Were we really saying good-bye to that pueblo? I know that my memory has taken residence there forever!

It was drizzling when we reached the city at midnight. The lights and neon signs sparkled on the wet pavement. The streets swarmed with people. At that late hour even children walked briskly, holding the hands of adults. And there were no soldiers with bayoneted rifles along the street.

The nurse kept checking my father's pulse and the feeding tube attached to his arm. Doctor Camacho was silent. He did not give my father much of his attention. He took Mama's, Ricardo's, and my blood pressure.

"You must understand, Margarita," he said at one point, "it's you and these children who matter now. I'm taking you to the hospital for observation."

"And Miguel?" But she did not look up, pleading for an answer, and went on dabbing her eyes with the handkerchief.

The sight of the ambulance, so linked with the military regime, caused heads to turn with annoyance. Twice we felt the impact of stones, and I saw a boy making an obscene gesture to the driver.

On every street corner were posters with the names of the new junta and the headlines with the promise of free elections.

As we advanced toward the center of the city, the shouts of "Freedom at last!" increased. I wanted to stick my head out of the window, to shout, above all shouting, "Victory belongs to my father. He gave his life for it!"

On Avenida Libertador men and women marched, arms linked, singing the national anthem. A man, standing on the steps surrounding the equestrian statue of Simón Bolívar, gesticulated, improvising a speech. A crowd around him clapped, cheering and waving small flags.

"This hysteria!" Doctor Camacho burst out with sudden anger. "It's a week now of this nonsense! How long will freedom last? What's the use!" His eyes darted toward the stretcher.

Ricardo and I looked at each other. "All this will not be in vain. The seeds of struggle will remain. . . . You'll see!" Those were his words, our father's, *un hombre indispensable.*

The ambulance slowed down. In front of us were the white walls and the lights of the hospital building.

ABOUT THE AUTHOR

Lyll Becerra de Jenkins grew up in Colombia. About *The Honorable Prison* she says: "My novel is a fusion of personal experience and invention."

The author's short stories have appeared in many periodicals and books throughout the world, including *The New York Times, The Boston Globe, Best American Short Stories,* and *The New Yorker*—where her story upon which *The Honorable Prison* is based was published. This is her first novel.

Ms. Jenkins, who has lived in the United States for more than twenty years, currently resides in Guilford, Connecticut, and teaches writing at Fairfield University. She and her husband have five children.